"Let him still be here," she whispered.

"Please let him be here." She felt as though she'd swallowed a double handful of goose feathers. She liked Joseph; she really did. And she wanted him to like her. She stopped short, seeing the empty swing. Her heart sank and her knees went weak.

And then she saw him on his knees beside the fishpond. "Joseph!" she called too loudly. She gave him her best smile as she hurried toward him.

"Ruby." He rose and stepped back from the edge of the pool.

"I brought you a drink," she said. "It's hot out here. I hope you like lemonade."

Joseph nodded. "*Ya*, I do." His lips curved in a tentative smile.

She'd remembered his amazing eyes, but memory wasn't as good as looking at him here in full daylight. They were as blue as cornflowers, intelligent, and they inspired trust. They were *Deitsch* blue eyes that seemed lit from within.

Was this the man her mother promised her would come?

Emma Miller lives quietly in her old farmhouse in rural Delaware. Fortunate enough to be born into a family of strong faith, she grew up on a dairy farm, surrounded by loving parents, siblings, grandparents, aunts, uncles and cousins. Emma was educated in local schools and once taught in an Amish schoolhouse. When she's not caring for her large family, reading and writing are her favorite pastimes.

Books by Emma Miller

Love Inspired

The Amish Matchmaker

A Match for Addy
A Husband for Mari
A Beau for Katie
A Love for Leah
A Groom for Ruby

Lancaster Courtships

The Amish Bride

Hannah's Daughters

Courting Ruth
Miriam's Heart
Anna's Gift
Leah's Choice
Redeeming Grace
Johanna's Bridegroom
Rebecca's Christmas Gift
Hannah's Courtship

Visit the Author Profile page at Harlequin.com for more titles.

A Groom for Ruby

Emma Miller

HARLEQUIN® LOVE INSPIRED®

Recycling programs
for this product may
not exist in your area.

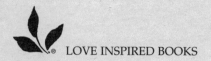

LOVE INSPIRED BOOKS

ISBN-13: 978-0-373-89944-9

A Groom for Ruby

Copyright © 2017 by Emma Miller

www.Harlequin.com

Printed in U.S.A.

Be kind to each other, tenderhearted,
forgiving one another, just as
God through Christ has forgiven you.
—*Ephesians* 4:32

Chapter One

Kent County, Delaware

"I'm sorry we couldn't have had a nicer day to greet you," the matchmaker said as she guided her driving horse onto a curving country lane. "We usually have beautiful weather in September."

Seated beside Sara Yoder on the buggy seat, Ruby nodded and clutched her black purse on her lap. She was too nervous to think of a sensible reply that wouldn't make her hostess believe she was a complete gooseberry. She'd been eager to come to Seven Poplars and had counted the weeks and days until her *mommi* and *daddi* had put her on the bus. But now that she was finally here, she was suddenly struck dumb.

Thunder rumbled overhead and heavy rain beat against the thin roof and sides of the buggy.

It was raining too hard for her to see much through the window over the dashboard. Sara's buggy was black, rather than gray like the ones she was used to, but otherwise it seemed completely familiar to be rolling along to the sound of the horse's hooves and the creak of the iron wheels. Her father had warned her that Seven Poplars was a more conservative Old Order Amish than their own community, but so far nothing in Sara's dress or manner of speaking had proved severe.

Still, Ruby had plenty of reason for concern. What if Sara didn't like her? Worse, what if Ruby didn't like any of the potential husbands that Sara offered? What if none of the men were interested in Ruby? She was twenty-five, a quarter of a century old. In a community where all of her friends and cousins her age had already married and were mothers or expecting babies, she was practically an old maid. If she failed to find someone, she'd be letting her parents down as well as herself.

All Ruby had ever dreamed of was a good husband, her own home and the opportunity to practice her faith under the loving eyes of her parents. But there would be no plump and laughing babies, no grandchildren for her mother and father, and no future for her if she couldn't find a husband. And not just any husband would do.

She wanted one who would love her with all his heart because, seeing the special relationship her parents had and the way each one had always put the other first, she wasn't willing to settle for less.

"We'll give you a few days to feel at home here, meet the other girls who are staying with me and then we'll talk about some possibilities," Sara explained.

Ruby nodded. She, who was rarely at a loss for words, felt as though she had a whole shoofly pie stuck in her throat. She swallowed, thinking she might be coming down with something. It had been raining since she'd left home; she'd gotten wet when she'd changed buses in Philadelphia and again when she'd gotten off in Dover. It wasn't cold out, but she felt damp and chilled, and her stomach had an ache that was either the greasy foot-long chili dog she'd bought from a cart in Philadelphia or she'd caught an ague. She pressed the back of her hand against her forehead, hoping that she wasn't feverish. Instead of being hot to the touch, her skin felt clammy, so it had to be nerves.

"I've already got someone in mind for you," Sara went on. "A widower only a few years older than you. He has a son, but your mother assured me that you would welcome a stepchild."

"Ya," Ruby managed. "Children are a heri-

tage from the Lord, offspring a reward from Him." She winced. Was that all she could say? Now she was imitating her bishop's wife, who was never content to speak for herself, but always had to be quoting proverbs so as to appear wiser than she was.

Not that Ruby didn't love children; she adored them. Since she had been young, she was always mothering orphaned animals, birds, even hapless insects that crossed her path. Once, she caused a ruckus during church service when the mouse she'd rescued from a cat wiggled out of her apron pocket and ran up Katie Brunstetter's leg.

"Here we are," Sara announced as she drove the horse into a yard. "And I promise, it all looks cheerier in the sunshine."

Through the rain, Ruby could make out a sprawling Cape Cod–style house and a white picket fence. Behind the house stood a tidy stable, painted white, and several well-kept outbuildings.

"This rain isn't going to let up. We'll have to make a run for it," Sara told her. "Leave your suitcase in the buggy. I'll have my hired man bring it in when he unharnesses the horse. Hiram won't mind and there's no sense in your struggling with it now."

A figure in a dark coat and hat dashed from

the house toward them. "That must be Hiram now," Sara said as she climbed down from the driver's seat and hurried toward the house. She paused only momentarily to exchange words with the man, then turned and waved. Ruby opened the door, peered down and saw a huge puddle.

Sara's hired man ran up to the buggy. He shouted something and held out his arms, but Ruby couldn't make out what he'd said above the din of the thunder and the rain pounding on the buggy's rooftop. "I don't need help, thanks," she called. The buggy was high. She wasn't very tall, so she knew that she'd have to give a little leap or she'd land smack in the middle of the mud puddle.

She forced a smile and hopped down.

At least, *that* was her intention. But the heel of her shoe caught on the edge of the buggy frame, and when she tried to catch her balance, her other foot caught in the hem of her dress. Having already reached the point of no return, her graceful hop to the ground became a lunge.

Which became a fall and Ruby felt herself sail through the air.

Sara's hired man darted forward and threw out his arms in an attempt to catch her. They collided. Hard. One second, Ruby felt herself hurling through the air and the next, she slammed into something solid. Her head smacked into the man's chin. His arms went around her, and the two of them crashed to the muddy ground with her on top of him. As they landed, there was a loud thump and a groan, and her would-be rescuer sagged backward with her full weight on top of him.

Arms and legs akimbo, Ruby rolled off the hired man into the puddle. Instantly, cold water soaked her stockings and skirt. She tried to get her balance by supporting herself with her left hand, but it slipped and she went facedown into the muck. Gasping, she scrambled up, intent on putting distance between her and Sara's hired man. She was mortified. She'd never live this down. How would she ever look the man in the eye? How could she face the matchmaker? Had any potential bride ever made such an embarrassing entrance to Sara's home?

Ruby glanced down at the man on the ground, steeling herself to meet an angry expression. But there was none. He hadn't moved. He lay there stretched on the ground with his eyes closed, his features slack, and the rain beating against his face. Ruby's heart leaped in her chest. Had she killed him? Crushed him beneath her weight? Ruby had what her mother called a *sturdy* frame. All the women on her mother's side were short and stocky.

"Are you hurt?" she yelled. And immediately felt a deep flush wash up her throat and face. Of course, he was hurt. Otherwise he wouldn't still be lying there in the pouring rain.

He lay there as motionless, as lifeless as the granite mounting block standing beside Sara's hitching post.

"Ach," Ruby wailed.

She dropped to her knees and lifted his head. His crumpled wool hat fell away. His face was as pale as buttermilk. His thick brown hair felt sticky to her touch. She jerked her hand back and stared at it, watching the rivulets of red rain. Not red rain. Blood. He was bleeding. A lot. Trickles of blood were running down out of his hair onto the grass. "Sara!" she shouted over her shoulder. "Sara! Come quick! I think I've killed your hired man!"

Joseph groaned and opened his eyes. A woman's beautiful face loomed over his. He gasped and let his eyes fall shut again. Where was he? He must be dreaming. He felt as if he were spinning and there was a throbbing ache in the back of his head. But he wanted to see those warm brown eyes again… He had to know if she was real or just his imagination.

"Hiram, wake up. You have to wake up," A

melodic, feminine voice urged. "Please don't die."
He felt her hands on his chest. "You can't die."

Hiram? Hiram was dying? Joseph drew in
a deep breath and forced his eyes open again.
What had happened to Hiram? And why was
he dreaming about Sara's hired man? Joseph
parted his lips and tried to speak, but soft fin-
gertips pressed against them.

"Hush, don't try to talk. Save your strength."
Save his strength? What for? He started to try
to sit up, but another wave of dizziness came
over him.

A cool hand pressed against his forehead.
"Everything's going to be all right," the voice
said. But who was this lovely girl? And why
was she so concerned about him?

"Who…who are you?" he managed to whisper.

"I'm Ruby. It's nice to meet you, Hiram."

What beautiful eyes she had. He'd never seen
such beautiful eyes. They were a warm brown,
almost the color of cinnamon, streaked with
darker ribbons of walnut. They radiated compassion. He could feel himself melting under
her gaze.

And her voice…

"Hiram?" he repeated thickly. "I'm not Hiram."

"Oh, Sara," the lovely girl said, speaking over
her shoulder. "He's hurt bad. He can't remember his own name."

Sara's chuckle cut through the fog in Joseph's head like a fresh breeze.

"That's not Hiram," Sara exclaimed. "This is one of my clients, Joseph Brenneman." The matchmaker came to stand over him.

Her voice faded and then came back to him. Joseph wasn't certain if only a moment had passed or an hour. But it was still raining. "I've called Hannah's daughter, Grace," the matchmaker said, holding an umbrella over him. "Emergency cell phone came in handy. You've got quite a bump there. Hit it on the edge of the brick flowerbed. I think you need to go into town for stitches. The immediate care clinic should be open. Be cheaper and faster than the hospital. I don't think you need an emergency room." This last statement seemed to be as much for herself as him.

"I need stitches?" Joseph reached back to gingerly touch his head, but all he could feel was cloth.

"Yes, you need stitches," the sweet voice chimed in. "Don't fuss with it. The towel is to stop the bleeding."

He blinked, trying to focus and then she was there again, the beautiful woman. "You're Ruby?" he asked. Where had she come from? Could this be the one Ellie had said that Sara had gone to pick up at the bus station? And then in bits and pieces, he remembered going out into the rain to help the women out of the buggy. The girl with the sweet voice had been getting down and… Had she fallen? She must have. Apparently, somehow, they'd fallen together. He stared at her, then lowered his gaze, overcome with shyness.

"I'm so sorry," she said. "It's all my fault."

"Ne." He slowly sat up, holding the wet towel against the back of his head. He wondered where his hat was. It wasn't proper for him to meet this lovely girl without his head covered. "I…I should have…have caught you." Joseph tried to remember what Ellie had said about her. Ruby. Even her name was special. Had Ellie said Ruby was coming to marry someone? Was she already spoken for?

Not that it would matter. Ruby would think him a hopeless woodenhead now, a klutz who'd slipped and broken his skull.

"Here's Grace now," Sara said. "We were in luck. She was just next door. She'll drive you into Dover and get you patched up." And then to Ruby, Sara explained, "Grace is my cousin's daughter. She's Mennonite and drives a car."

"I don't think I need to see a doctor," Joseph protested. "It's just a little bump on the head." He raised his gaze to Ruby again.

Sara scoffed. "Nonsense. You cracked your

head like a melon. You need more stitches than I'd like to put in you. And you're not to worry about the cost. You fell in my yard, and I'll pay for everything."

"Do you feel well enough to walk?" Grace appeared at his side, taking his arm.

"I can walk," Joseph said.

"I'm going with him." Ruby grabbed his other arm to help him to his feet. "It's the least I can do."

Sara looked at her. "Are you certain? Not sure how long the wait will be."

"*Ne*, I want to," Ruby insisted.

"Well, then, go and change your dress and stockings. There's no need for you to go out with your things wet and dirty," Sara replied. "You look as if you've been swimming in a mud puddle."

"I'll hurry," Ruby said.

Walking to Grace's motor vehicle took more effort than Joseph expected. Every step he took was a shaky one. His stomach churned and his head throbbed. He felt foolish with the towel on his head. As they made their way to the black SUV, he remembered his horse and buggy. He'd come to see Sara, and his horse was still harnessed and tied in her shed. "My horse," he began, but Sara patted his hand.

"Don't worry. Hiram will take care of him. Plenty of room in my barn."

"He's wet," Joseph said.

"I said you're not to worry." She peered into his face. "Hiram can rub him down and give him a nice ration of oats."

Joseph slid into the back seat and leaned back, gratefully resting his aching head. He thought he only closed his eyes for a moment but then the door on the other side opened and Ruby climbed in. "It will be all right," she said soothingly.

A short time later, they arrived at the urgent care facility and Joseph, Sara and Ruby got out of the car.

"I'll call you when we need a ride home," Sara told Grace. "No telling how long a wait we'll have." She turned to Joseph as they went through the automatic doors at the entrance. "You two just find a seat in the waiting room. I'll check you in. Hopefully, they'll see you soon."

But the walk-in facility was busy and it was obvious he wasn't going to see a doctor right away. Instead, Ruby guided him to a corner of the crowded room while Sara checked him in. Ruby found two empty seats side by side and proceeded to convince another waiting patient and his mother into moving to the far wall so that Sara could sit with her and Joseph. As Joseph watched Ruby, he couldn't help but be surprised a young woman could be so assertive with *Englishers* in a strange town.

"You'll be able to see the television better from over there," Ruby assured the woman who was wearing a tight Superman T-shirt, cut-off denim shorts and cowboy boots.

Her child, a stout, red-faced boy of about eight, didn't appear to be too sick to Joseph. In one hand the boy clutched a can of soda, in the other a bag of chips. But he was whining that he was hungry and needed a candy bar from the vending machine. The kid's head was shaved except for a standing ridge down the center, two inches high and a thin braid hanging down the back of his dirty shirt.

"You'll be closer to the snacks, as well," Ruby said with a cheery smile as she scooped up the woman's rain jacket and handed it to her. The boy's mother reluctantly gathered her belongings and moved toward the other vacant seats. "Terrible, isn't it, how you have to wait?" Ruby went on. "We're so grateful that you were kind enough to allow our friend to sit with us."

"I want a candy bar!" the boy whined.

"All right, all right," the woman said as she and her son walked away.

Joseph glanced at Ruby as she plopped her

black purse on the empty seat on one side of him and sat down in the other one. He wanted to tell her how much he admired her ability to deal with the situation, but as usual, words failed him. All that he could manage was, "Your English is *goot.* I mean *good.*"

To his delight, she turned that sweet smile on him. "Thank you."

Joseph felt his face grow warm and he averted his eyes.

"My *mommi* and *daddi* thought it was important that I learn English early on. Most parents from our church send their little ones off to school not knowing a single word, but not my *mam* and *dat.* Not my parents. No, indeed…"

Joseph stole a glimpse of Ruby as she chattered on. Usually, when he was with a girl, he was too nervous to get out a sensible word. He liked girls; he desperately wanted a wife. A family. He just wasn't good at meeting girls. Talking to them.

Ruby asked him a question, but then thankfully went on, not waiting for him to come up with a clever reply. She just kept talking and he kept staring at her, not even trying to hide his infatuation now.

Joseph couldn't believe this was happening. If he'd known that falling and cracking his head would have gotten him the attention of a beautiful young woman, he would have done it long ago. Best of all, Ruby wasn't blaming him. She seemed to think that it was *her* fault. And she didn't appear to care whether he talked or not. She seemed to have no problem talking for them both.

Joseph glanced up and saw Sara, who had taken the seat Ruby had saved for her, looking at them. He wondered what she was thinking. Did she think he was slow-witted because Ruby was talking and he wasn't? Some people who didn't know him well thought he was slow. Even his mother agonized over his lack of knowing what to say when girls were nearby. "Speak up," she always told him. When he was a boy, it was "Stand up straight, Joseph. Look people in the eye when they speak to you. Do you want the teacher to think you have an over-ripe cucumber for a brain?" And now that he was a man full grown, it was "God gave you a mind. Why can't you show it when it matters most?"

Joseph became aware that Ruby had stopped speaking. He looked into her eyes and was rewarded with another compassionate smile. She was waiting for him to say something, but what? He tried to think. What had she been saying?

He was so overwhelmed by her presence that he was at a total loss. And just when he thought the floor would open and swallow him up, Sara came to his rescue.

"Ruby comes to us from Lancaster County in Pennsylvania," Sara said, handing Ruby her purse. "I've promised her parents that I'll find her a match."

"Who is it?" he blurted. Was it Levi King? Jason Bontrager? If she'd set her *kapp* for either of them, he wouldn't have the chance of a pullet in a fox den. Levi could charm the birds from the trees. And Jason had a blacksmith's shoulders and a father with more farms than he had sons.

"She's not spoken for yet," Sara said. "But I'm certain it won't be long before we'll all be invited to her wedding."

Ruby blushed prettily.

Then Sara added icing to the cake by saying, "Our Joseph is looking for a bride. He's a master mason, and is a credit to his mother and community."

"Is your father living?" Ruby asked. "*Ach*, maybe I shouldn't have asked that. I have a wonderful father." Without taking a breath, she switched from smooth and perfect English to *Deitsch*. "He's so good to me. And he loves to laugh. Everyone says I look like my mother but I'm most like my father. I hope that if I do find someone to wed, we won't live far from my parents. I'm devoted to them."

She paused and looked at him expectantly. What was he supposed to say?

"Joseph's father died when he was very young," Sara said. She reached into her bag and pulled out a Christian romance novel. "I hope the two of you won't mind, but I'm dying to see what happens in my book."

"Do you like to read?" Ruby asked Joseph as Sara settled in her chair.

He nodded. Instantly, his head began to throb again and it was all he could do not to reach up to touch the towel. But he didn't want her to think he was a complainer or that he wasn't tough.

"Don't move," Ruby cautioned, brushing her hand against his wet sleeve. "I don't want you to start bleeding again. I feel so terrible that you were hurt. And I'm entirely to blame. I'm such a klutz. You may as well know it. I've always been a klutz."

"I read," he managed. "The Bible. And *The Budget*."

"Your injury will probably be written up in *The Budget*. I hope no one mentions my name.

It's so embarrassing. And you'll probably miss work. Will your boss be angry with you?"

"*Ne*. I…I'm sort of an independent contractor."

"You are? That's wonderful." She clasped her hands together. They were nice hands. "What kind of masonry do you do? Bricklaying? Stonework? Cement?"

"*Ya*. All."

"And you're a master mason already? You must do fine work."

"I try."

She smiled at him. "Listen to me. When I'm nervous, I talk too much." She chuckled. "Truth is, I always talk too much. Are you thirsty? Hungry? There are vending machines over there. The least I can do is to buy you a drink. Wait, I'll go see what they have." She got up, taking her purse with her, and threaded her way through the waiting people to the corner.

Sara glanced at him. The corners of her mouth were drawn up in a "cat that swallowed the cream" hint of a smile. "Ruby talks a lot, doesn't she?"

"Not too much," Joseph defended, watching Ruby. "Just the right amount, I think."

Ruby returned. "They have Coke, orange, lemon-lime and root beer. Then there's bottled water and iced tea in a can. What would you like?"

Joseph reached for his wallet.

"Ne," Ruby said firmly, patting her purse. "This is my treat. I insist."

"All right." Feeling bold, he returned her smile and said, "Next time, I pay."

"But what would you like?" she asked.

"Soda is good."

"But what kind?"

He shrugged. "Anything wet."

She giggled. *"Ne*, you have to tell me what you like best."

"R-root beer," he managed. "I like root beer."

The smile spread across her face, making her even more beautiful. "Me too. I love it. My *daddi* says that I like it too well. It's not good for my teeth. But I drink it anyway."

Her teeth looked fine to him. White and even and sparkling.

"And now you get to choose a snack. Pretzels. Chips. Candy. Or peanut butter crackers."

"Crackers," he said. "I like…crackers."

"Me too." She laughed, looking down at him like he was the cleverest man she had ever met. "Isn't that funny? We both like the same treats. Sara, I'm not forgetting you. What would you like?"

Sara glanced up from her book. "I'm fine.

Too many treats and I'll grow out of my clothes. You young people enjoy your snacks."

"If you're sure," Ruby said, turning back to Joseph. "I'll be right back with your soda and crackers."

As she walked away, he noticed that she was wearing a green dress. He liked green. He smiled to himself as he watched her. His head hurt and he was still feeling a little dazed, but it didn't matter because this was turning out to be the best day of his life.

Chapter Two

Joseph pushed back his plate. He'd eaten only a few bites of potato salad and nibbled at a fried chicken leg. The truth was the back of his head where he'd gotten the stitches stung and he didn't have much of an appetite. And he had more on his mind than eating.

"Joseph, you've barely put a thing in your mouth." His mother's delicate forehead wrinkled with concern. "I knew you should have stayed in bed this morning. Does your head hurt? Are you dizzy?" She fluttered her hands helplessly over her plate. For a small woman, Joseph was always amazed at how much his mother could eat and never gain an extra pound.

He forced a smile and took a sip of the glass of buttermilk next to his plate. Normally, he loved buttermilk, but today, it tasted flat on his tongue. "Now, don't fuss. A few stitches. Nothing for you to worry yourself over."

His mother rose, came around the table and pressed a cool palm to his forehead. "You feel a little warm to me. You might be running a fever."

"*Ne*, no fever," he protested. "It's a hot day. Near ninety, I'd guess. And you've made enough food for two families." It was stifling there in the kitchen. All the windows were open, but no breeze stirred the plain white curtains. It made a man think longingly of cool autumn mornings.

His mother, Magdalena, nibbled at her lower lip. "It wouldn't hurt for you to go back to the doctor."

Joseph raised a hand in protest. "Mother, *ne*, really. There's no need for you to be concerned. I slipped in the mud and knocked my head. It's nothing. I've had far worse. Remember when I fell out of the hayloft?"

"And landed in the pile of manure your father had just forked out of the cow stall," she finished for him with a chuckle. "At least you had no stitches then."

"No stitches, but I broke my arm in two places."

"We felt so awful." She shook her head ruefully. "My only *kinder*, my precious seven-year-old son in so much pain. We rushed you to the hospital and there you were all covered in muck and stinking like an outhouse with all them *Englishers* staring at us. Such a bad mother, they must have thought, to have no care for her child."

They traded smiles at the shared memory. He'd long ago forgotten the hurt of the broken arm. What he remembered was that he'd gone all that summer unable to swim in the pond with his friends, and that his father and mother had churned ice cream for him every Saturday. He wiped his eyes with the napkin, rubbing away the tears of laughter and maybe something more. That summer and the taste of that sweet ice cream on his tongue were some of the last memories he had of his father. His *dat* had been killed in a farming accident that September.

His mother was still hovering, something she had a tendency to do. "Maybe you could manage a slice of pie?" she coaxed. "Peach. Your favorite. I made it especially for you."

Which was what she said of most meals... "Save it all for supper tonight," Joseph answered. "I've got an errand to run this afternoon, and I'll be sure to be hungry later. We'll have everything cold, and you won't even have to heat up the kitchen by turning on the stove." His mother pursed her lips and began clearing away the dishes. Her silence and the pained expression on her face was an obvious sign of her disapproval.

"Can I help you clean up?" he offered.

She shook her head. "This is my job, Joseph. It's the least I can do, being a widow and dependent on your charity."

Joseph bit back the retort that this house was hers as long as she lived and he loved her and would never consider her a burden. He'd said that many times before. Instead, he rose to put the milk and chicken into the refrigerator.

Theirs was a small kitchen for an Amish house, but it provided everything his mother needed to cook and preserve food from her garden. He'd worked hard since he was fifteen to provide for the two of them, and his *mam* had done her share by keeping their home as shiny as a new penny. The Bible said to honor your mother and father, and he tried to always remember that when she was being difficult.

There'd never been any doubt in Joseph's mind that she loved him and wanted what was best for him. Twice she could have remarried, but both times she'd refused, even though both prospective husbands could have given her a more spacious home and an easier life. "A stepfather might be harsh on you," she'd said. "And your needs might be lost in a large family of stepbrothers and stepsisters. We're better on our own."

Joseph smiled at her as he crossed the room to take his hat from the peg near the door. It fit a little snug because the emergency room doctor had shaved the back of his head and covered the six stitches with a thick bandage. But he could hardly show up at the matchmaker's without his head covered. It wouldn't be proper.

"Where are you going?" His mother removed the plate of chicken from the refrigerator where he'd just put it and covered it with a clean length of cheesecloth before placing it back in the refrigerator. "I think you'd best put your errand off for a few days," she said. "No need for you to go out in this afternoon heat."

"I'll be fine," Joseph assured her. "I won't be long."

"Where did you say you were going?" She dropped her hands to her hips and tilted her head in that way she always did that reminded him of a curious little wren. Her bright blue eyes narrowed. "Joseph?"

"I didn't say." He opened the back door. "I'll be back in plenty of time to milk the cow before supper."

"But Joseph—"

He closed the door behind him and kept walking. He loved his mother dearly, but if he let her have her way, she'd treat him as though he was twelve years old and not in his late twenties. He was blessed to have a mother who loved him so much, but she had a strong will, and it was sometimes a struggle as to who was the head of their house. She was sensitive, and if he was too firm with her, she'd dissolve in tears. He couldn't stand the idea of making his mother cry and he felt relieved that she hadn't wept when he hadn't done what she'd wanted and stayed home.

Turning to a matchmaker to find him a wife had been his mother's idea, and after hearing her talk about it for nearly two years, he'd weakened and agreed to let Sara Yoder see if she would have more success than he had on his own. He'd been reluctant and more than a little nervous because he'd always been tongue-tied around young women. He'd never imagined that he'd meet anyone like Ruby so quickly or in such an unusual way.

Whistling, Joseph descended the porch steps. Glancing back over his shoulder, he caught a glimpse of white curtain moving at a window. As he'd suspected, his mother was watching him. He strode around the house to his mother's flowerbed, out of her sight, and quickly picked a bouquet of colorful blooms. A girl like Ruby probably had lots of fellows saying sweet stuff to her, but girls liked flowers. Maybe they could speak for him.

Everyone talked about his mother's skill at growing flowers. She had beds of them that brightened the front yard and clustered around the house. She rarely cut them for the house, but from early spring to late autumn she had beautiful bouquets to sell at Spence's Auction. He didn't claim to know much about them other than to turn over the soil when she asked him or to fertilize and weed the beds, but he'd seen her create enough bouquets to know what flowers went with each other. For Ruby, he chose a rainbow of cosmos, sweet peas, zinnias and asters. He cradled the stems in peat moss and wrapped them in green florist's paper just as he'd seen his mother do for her stand at Spence's Market. He still had the headache, but he was whistling as he hitched up his driving horse to the cart.

All the way to Sara's house, Joseph tried to think of something sensible to say to Ruby when he gave her the flowers. He even practiced saying the words aloud. It wasn't difficult to be clever when there was no one to hear him but the horse. Should he speak to her in *Deitsch* or English? She'd told him that she was from Pennsylvania. Those Amish up there were less conservative. Maybe she'd think he was old-fashioned if he spoke *Deitsch*. So English. But what did he say?

"A little something to welcome you to Seven Poplars." That was good, but should it be "*welcome* you" or "welcome *you*"? What word should he emphasize? Or maybe that would sound too put-on. They'd talked a lot in the urgent care waiting room. If he welcomed her, it might appear that he was acting like she was just another of Sara's clients and she wasn't special.

Joseph's stomach flip-flopped. He felt a little light-headed. His head still hurt, but he didn't think that was the cause of his distress. The truth was, he was scared. His mouth was dry and it was hard to think straight. He'd always heard of love striking a man like lightning cutting down a tree, but he'd never believed it until now. Ruby Plank falling into his arms was the most exciting thing that had ever happened to him and he didn't want to mess it up.

The trouble was, when it came to girls, he always did. And he was terrified that this time would be no different. Joseph was still going over and over in his mind what he would say as he approached Sara Yoder's back door. The yard had been quiet, without anyone in sight, and he couldn't hear any talking from inside. Sara's house was usually bustling with young people coming and going, but today he didn't see so much as a dragonfly hovering over the flowerbeds along the drive. What if he'd come to find that some other fellow had taken Ruby buggy riding? Or worse, what if she'd changed her mind about making a match after yesterday's disaster and returned to Pennsylvania?

Gathering his courage, he knocked on the wooden screen door. No one appeared, so he knocked again, and then called out in *Deitsch*. "Hello? Is anybody to home?" Again, there was only silence except for a bee that had gotten trapped on the screen porch and was buzzing loudly as it attempted to escape.

Joseph's stomach turned over. Now his head was really hurting. He was hot and sweaty, and he'd crossed his mother and come here hoping to see Ruby again. All for nothing. But he wasn't ready to give up yet. Maybe they were in the garden and hadn't heard him. He left the porch and circled around the house. In the side yard, farthest from the drive, was a wooden swing, a brick walk, a fishpond and a fountain. "Hello?" he called again.

And then he stopped short. There was a blanket spread on the clover near the tiny pond. A young woman lay stretched out on her stomach, bare ankles crossed, apparently lost in a book. But the most startling thing to Joseph was her hair. Among the Amish, a woman's hair was always covered. Little girls wore pigtails with baby caps or student *kapps*. Teenage girls and women of all ages pinned their hair up in a bun and covered it with a scarf or a prayer *kapp*.

This woman was clearly Amish because she wore a sky blue dress with a dark apron over it. Black leather shoes stood beside the blanket with black stockings tossed beside them. But the woman's hair wasn't pinned up under a *kapp* or covered with a scarf. It rippled in a thick shimmering mane down the back of her neck and over her shoulders nearly to her waist.

Joseph's mouth gaped. He clutched the bouquet of flowers so tightly between his hands that he distinctly heard several stems snap. He swallowed, unable to stop staring at her beautiful hair. It was brown, but brown in so many shades…tawny and russet…the color of shiny acorns in winter and the hue of ripe wheat. He knew he shouldn't be staring. He'd intruded on a private moment, seen what he shouldn't. He should turn and walk away. But he couldn't.

He inhaled deeply. "Hello," he stammered. "I'm sorry, I was looking for—"

"Ach!" The young woman rose on one elbow and twisted to face him. It was Ruby. Her eyes widened in surprise. "Joseph?"

"*Ya*. It's me." He struggled to think of something else sensible to say.

Ruby sat up, dropping her paperback onto the blanket, pulling her knees up and tucking her feet under her skirt. "I was drying my hair," she said. "I washed it. I still had mud in it from last night."

Joseph grimaced. "Sorry."

"*Ne*." She shook her head. "It was all my fault."

"An accident," he said.

"And you had to get stitches. Are you in pain?"

He shook his head.

"*Goot*. I was worried about you."

He tried not to smile, but the thought that she'd worried about him filled him with hope.

"Everyone else went to Byler's store." She blushed prettily and covered her face with her hands. "But I stayed home. To wash my hair. What must you think of me without my *kapp*?" Her words were apologetic, but her tone was mischievous, rather than guilty. Dropping her hands, she chuckled.

She had a merry laugh, Joseph thought, a laugh as beautiful and unique as she was. She was regarding him with definite interest. Her eyes were the shade of cinnamon splashed with swirls of chocolate, large and thickly lashed. His mouth went dry.

She smiled encouragingly.

He shrugged. A dozen thoughts tumbled in his mind: he could comment about the color of her dress or ask her what she was reading or say something about the weather, but nothing seemed like the right thing to say. "I…I never know what to say to pretty girls," he admitted as he tore his gaze away from hers. "You must think I'm thickheaded." He shuffled his feet. "I'll come back another time when—"

"Who are those flowers for?" Ruby asked. "Did you bring them for Sara?"

"*Ne*, not Sara." Joseph's face grew hot. He tried to say "I brought them for you," but again the words stuck in his throat. Dumbly, he held them out to her. Several of the asters in the bouquet had broken stems and they hung down awkwardly. It took every ounce of his courage not to turn and run.

She scrambled to her feet, her smile as sweet as sunrise on a winter day, her beautiful eyes sparkling with pleasure. *"Danki,"* she said as she reached for the bouquet. "I love flowers. Nobody ever brought me flowers before." She clutched them to her. "I think they're wonderful."

For a long moment, they stood staring at each other. Ruby's hair tumbled down around her shoulders, still damp from the washing, the thick locks gleaming in the sunlight. Her hair looked so soft that he wanted to touch it, to feel the curls spring between his fingers.

Joseph stepped back another step and sucked in a breath of air. They were practically strangers. He shouldn't be here with her without a chaperone. He shouldn't be looking at her unbound hair. It was scandalous. If anyone found out, there would be talk. He couldn't do that to Ruby. "I g-guess I should go," he blurted. "I shouldn't... We shouldn't—"

"Ne," she said. "Don't go yet. Wait here. No, sit there." She waved toward the wooden swing. It was fashioned of cedar, suspended on a sturdy frame and shaded by a latticework canopy. "Where it's cooler. Wait there. I'll be right back." She ran several yards, then turned and ran back. "Stay right there," she repeated before grabbing up everything in the blanket and dashing around the house.

Stunned, Joseph did as she said. Truthfully, it was good to get off his feet and when he gave a small push, the motion of the swing eased the tension in his neck and shoulders. What had he been thinking to come here this afternoon? To bring flowers for Ruby? But he'd had to come. He couldn't get her off his mind. But he'd never expected her to be so sweet. He closed his eyes and thought about how pretty her unbound hair was.

Ruby slammed the kitchen door shut behind her. *"Ya!"* she exclaimed joyfully. *"Ya!"* Laughing, she spun around in a circle and buried her face in the flowers. Joseph had come back! She'd been certain that knocking him nearly senseless and sending him to the hospital had ruined any chance she might have had of attracting the respectable young mason. But, in spite of her clumsiness, he'd returned and brought her flowers. It was almost too good to be true. She couldn't wait to tell her mother.

But Joseph had caught her in the yard, sprawled out on a blanket with her hair wet and hanging instead of being decently covered with her *kapp*, she reminded herself. He'd been shocked. Probably he'd come in search of one of the other girls and only given her the flowers to be kind. But he was kind. And not only good-looking, but sweet natured and clearly in search of a wife. She didn't dare let herself hope that he might choose her, but neither could she throw away any opportunity she might have.

Her mother's words of advice came to her as clearly as if her *mommi* were here in this room with her. *You will find someone who will see your inner beauty, Ruby. And he will be the one who deserves you.*

Coming to Sara Yoder's and asking the matchmaker to find her a husband had been an act of desperation. Her parents had believed that the only way for her to find someone was to go to a place where no one knew her. And now Joseph had fallen into her lap. Or, rather, she'd fallen into his. She couldn't let him slip through her fingers. He might not be someone that she wanted to marry, but she couldn't know that until they were better acquainted.

Dropping the flowers into the sink, she searched for a container to put them in. Spying an old blue-and-white-speckled bowl and pitcher on a table in the adjoining room, she snatched up the pitcher, dumped the flowers in and filled the pitcher half-full of water. She left the arrangement on the counter and ran upstairs to her bedroom to make herself decent.

Grabbing a brush, she raked it though her damp hair, twisted the mass into a knot and pinned it securely at the back of her head. She snatched up her *kapp* and took the stairs to the first floor two at a time. What if Joseph hadn't stayed in the yard? What if he'd examined the book she'd been reading and discovered that it was one of Sara's romance novels? Would he think she was flighty?

Breathlessly, she filled glasses with ice and lemonade and hurried back outside. "Let him still be here," she whispered. "Please let him be here." She felt as though she'd swallowed a double handful of goose feathers. She liked Joseph; she really did. And she wanted him to like her. She stopped short, seeing the empty swing. Her heart sank and her knees went weak.

And then she saw him on his knees beside the fishpond. "Joseph!" she called too loudly. She gave him her best smile as she hurried toward him.

"Ruby." He rose and stepped back from the lip of the pool. "Her fish are getting big," he said. "I saw an orange-and-black one." Joseph's hat was crooked, and she could see that it was too tight due to the bulky bandage.

"I brought you a drink," she said. "It's hot out here. I hope you like lemonade."

Joseph nodded. "*Ya*, I do." His lips curved in a tentative smile.

She'd been with him all evening, here at the house and at the hospital, but she hadn't really gotten a good look at him. She'd remembered his amazing eyes, but memory wasn't as good as looking at him here in full daylight. They were as blue as cornflowers, intelligent, and they inspired trust. They were *Deitsch* blue eyes that seemed lit from within. He wasn't a huge man, but neither was he small. He was exactly the right size, she decided, tall enough without being gangly, and broad at the shoulders without appearing muscle-bound. Joseph's nose was straight and well formed, and he had a smattering of freckles across his rosy cheeks.

Was this the man her mother promised her would come?

Joseph reached for the glass.

Suddenly, she was aware that she'd been staring at him, lost in her own thoughts while he was waiting for his cold drink. She shoved the lemonade at him with too much force. As his hand closed around the glass, ice and liquid splashed across the front of his shirt.

"Ne!" she protested. "I'm so sorry."

Joseph looked down at his shirt and laughed. "That's one way to cool me off."

"It's all my fault," she said. "I'm such a klutz."

"My fault. I was looking at you and not the glass."

Ruby shook her head. She felt sick. "You might as well know I always trip or drop or knock over things. I always have. When I was in school, the teacher called me stumble-bumble. I never got to write on the blackboard because I either snapped off the chalk or dropped the eraser and then kicked it when

I leaned over to pick it up or—" She gestured, showing him the hopelessness of the situation.

"Yeah, well…did you ever get up in front of the whole school and the parents and…and…not be able to say your own name?" Joseph asked.

"You didn't," she exclaimed.

"I…I did." He paused and then went on. "It was our Christmas party. I was supposed to recite a poem. It was short, just six lines. But I couldn't get past my name. I just stood there like a block of wood with my mouth open, trying not to cry."

Ruby pressed her lips together. "I know what you mean. It's bad when I tip over the milk bucket or catch my apron in the barn door, but it's worse when people are watching."

He shook his head. "Anyone can have an accident."

"But I make a regular habit of it."

"Then I'd best take that other glass before you dump it over my head," he teased.

For an instant, she thought he was mocking her, but when she saw the expression on his face, she was certain she'd made a friend. She gave him her lemonade and followed him sheepishly to the swing.

"You…you sit first," Joseph said.

She could feel herself blushing, but she didn't feel as though she was going to throw up anymore. She felt happy. She'd sent him to the hospital with a broken head and she'd tried to drown him in lemonade, and he didn't seem to care. He was smiling at her the way she'd seen other boys smile at the girls they wanted to drive home from singings.

"Admit it," he said. "You've never been at a loss for words."

Ruby shook her head as he handed her lemonade to her. "Words I have aplenty," she said. "Too many according to some people. My grandfather used to say that I talked faster than a horse could trot." She sighed. "I've tried to stop and think before I speak, but the words bubble up inside me, and when I open my mouth they fly out."

"I don't think you talk too much," Joseph pronounced solemnly. "I like to hear you talk." He chuckled. "It keeps me from having to try and keep up my end of the conversation."

She gazed down at her drink and considered what he'd just said. She took a sip of the lemonade. It was a little tart.

Joseph took a seat beside her. There was a gap between them, not too much, and not too little. They were far enough apart to satisfy propriety. "I have more work than I can do," he said. "Bricklaying. Cement. Fireplaces."

She held her breath.

"I asked Sara to try to find me a wife."

Ruby's heartbeat quickened.

"And...and I know that's why you're staying with Sara." He met her gaze. "To...to find a husband, I mean, not to find a wife."

She smiled at him, thinking he was the cutest thing she'd ever seen.

"If you don't have anyone either, maybe—" he swallowed, and his fingers tightened on the glass "—I thought... I mean... I hoped we..."

"Could see if we suit each other?" she finished for him.

Joseph nodded eagerly.

"I'd like that," she said. "I'd like that very much."

"Me too," he agreed. He looked down. "But... I suppose I... It's only fair I should tell you I... I have a good trade and I work hard, but I'm far from well-off. And...and you should know that I have a widowed mother that I'm responsible for." He spread his hands. "I'm a plain... plain man, Ruby. If that's not what you're looking for..."

She clapped her hands together and smiled at him. "That's exactly what I'm looking for, Joseph Brenneman. I think we'll suit each other very well."

Chapter Three

"It…it's early. I…I know," Joseph said, hat in hand at Sara's back door. It was Wednesday morning, and he was starting a foundation for the Moses King family's addition today. He had a lot of work to do. But he couldn't wait any longer to speak to the matchmaker. "Could I? That is…is…" As usual, the words he wanted to say caught in his throat, choking him. He could feel his face growing hot. Sara would think him a fool. Maybe she was right.

Sara stepped out onto the porch in her bare feet. She was a round, tidy woman with crinkly dark hair, and dark eyes that seemed to bore through him. "Ruby isn't here," she said. "She went off with Ellie to the schoolhouse. Ellie's our teacher. Today is their first day, and Ruby offered to give her a hand getting the first graders settled in."

"Didn't come to—" He broke off when he realized that he was practically shouting at Sara in an effort to get the words out. "Came to see you." The last bit came in a rush, like shelled peas popping out of a shell all at once. He groaned inwardly. Why was this so hard? Words rolled off his cousin Andy's tongue so easily. Tyler never seemed to have trouble talking to women. Joseph took a deep breath. "I want…" He swallowed the lump in his throat. "Ruby. Make a match. You. With us."

Sara's shrewd face softened. "This sounds serious, Joseph. Maybe you'd best come to my office. I don't like to discuss business in front of other people. I like to keep things confidential until matches are formally announced. To give everyone privacy."

Joseph nodded and tugged on the brim of his straw work hat. He'd shaved and showered that morning. It was important to look his best. He might sound like a hayseed, but there was no need to look like one. He'd even worn a new shirt his mother just made him, but he had an old one in the buggy that he could change into when he got to the King house. If he ruined this one with concrete, his mother would not be happy, and when she wasn't happy, home could be an unpleasant place. But the shirt didn't matter now. It was what he had to get straight with Sara.

"Ruby," he blurted. Her name came out in a whisper, which he corrected in a deep and more insistent tone. "Ruby. I…I want to talk to you about…" He looked down at his boots. "Her," he finished in a rush of breath.

When he looked up, a hint of a smile lit Sara's almond-shaped eyes, but her mouth remained firm. After a second's hesitation, she held open the door and motioned him into the kitchen.

A tall girl in a lilac dress was washing dishes at the sink while an even prettier one dried. The tall one turned to smile at him. "Arlene," Sara said, "This is Joseph Brenneman. Leah, I think you know each other."

"Hello, Joseph," Leah said. "It's good to see you again." And then to Arlene, "Joseph's from another church district, but we used to see each other at auctions and work frolics."

Arlene nodded. Smiled.

"Ya." Joseph's cheeks burned with embarrassment. Leah had once hit a home run when he was pitching at an interschool game. She'd married a Mennonite and gone to South America to be a missionary. He'd died and now Leah had come back to Seven Poplars; she was staying with the matchmaker. Leah had always been known as the beauty of the county and she'd been nice too. But he'd never been drawn to her, not even as a boy still wet behind the ears.

"Ruby," he managed. "I...came for Ruby. About Ruby," he corrected. "A match...with Ruby. Maybe," he added. "I hope," he clarified.

Arlene chuckled. "I see," she replied in *Deitsch*.

She wore a different-style *kapp* than Leah and the other local girls, a shape of prayer covering Joseph wasn't familiar with. Ruby did too, but hers wasn't like Arlene's. Ruby's was heart shaped. He decided that he liked Ruby's *kapp* better.

Thankfully, Sara rescued him from having to say anything else by leading him through the kitchen to her office. Sara gestured to a chair in front of and facing a desk. She closed the door and took a seat behind the desk. The desktop was empty except for a spiral notebook and a black pen.

Joseph leaned forward in his chair. The windows were open, but with the door closed there wasn't any breeze and it was warm in here. Unconsciously, he ran a finger under his collar. Sara was just sitting there, looking at him. He couldn't have been more uncomfortable if she'd caught him chopping wood without his shirt. "I want...want to court Ruby," he declared bluntly.

"So I gather." Sara sat back and smiled. "This is a little sudden, don't you think? You've known each other, what? Three days? And that's including today, and I don't think you've even seen her today." Her eyes sparkled with amusement rather than disapproval.

Joseph shifted in his chair. It was straight backed, oak and had probably been made at the chair shop not half a mile away. His mouth felt dry and he was slightly light-headed. *"Ya, but..."* He exhaled. But what? How did he explain to Sara that how long they'd known each other had nothing to do with anything? That he'd known the moment he'd opened his eyes, lying flat out in Sara's driveway, that Ruby was the girl for him.

Sara's chuckle became a full-throated laugh. It was a jolly laugh for a woman and it came up from deep in her chest and bubbled out with genuine mirth.

Joseph stood up. He wasn't going to sit here and be laughed at.

"Sit down, sit down," Sara insisted, waving her hand at him. "I wasn't laughing at you. I was surprised. But in a good way, Joseph. I'm just not used to young men being in such a hurry." She laced her fingers together, leaned forward and rested her hands on the desktop. "Don't you want to get to know Ruby a little before you start talking about marriage?"

"Ne." He shook his head, settling in the chair

again. "She's the one. For me." He forced himself to meet Sara's piercing gaze. "I like Ruby."

"You've made that clear." Sara's attitude grew kindly as she slipped on a pair of wire-frame glasses she'd retrieved from her apron pocket. "And it's clear that you're uncomfortable here with me. I'm sorry for that. I hope you can come to think of me as a friend, maybe a favorite aunt. I like you, Joseph. You appear to be a fine man and an excellent candidate for one of my brides-to-be. You're just the sort of man I like to find, someone who isn't wishy-washy, someone who knows his own mind." She paused and opened her notebook. She thumbed through until she'd reached a page about half-way through and picked up her pen. She jotted something down and then made eye contact with him again. "Sorry. I have a system, and if I don't keep to it, I'd forget who was who."

"Ruby's not spoken for, is she?" That was the question he'd been dreading to ask. He knew he'd asked Sara that before, but he was afraid that someone had snapped her up since then. Because if there were another suitor, there'd be a whole lot more trouble before things could get worked out. He wasn't going to give up. Sara had promised she could find him a wife; he just had to make her understand that Ruby was the one for him.

"Well…" Sara tapped her notebook with her pen. "I'd planned to introduce her to a blacksmith." She looked up. "And I'd wanted you to get to know Arlene. I think you'd be very compatible. But if you've seen Ruby and you're taken with her, there's no reason why the two of you shouldn't—"

"Then you have no problem matching us?"

Sara separated her hands and raised them, palms forward. "Now, just slow down, Joseph. It's customary for my couples to take this one step at a time—get to know each other before a match is actually made. Usually couples attend some singings together, have meals here at the house and see each other at church. Picking a wife or a husband is a serious matter."

He dropped his straw hat onto his knee and balled his hands into fists. They seemed clumsy, like two clubs rather than hands and he tucked them under his knees. His right foot wanted to bounce on his heel like he did when he was nervous but he forced it firmly to the floor and held it there by force of will. He was sweating. He could feel tiny beads of moisture trickling down the back of his shirt. Sara was looking at him expectantly. She was waiting for him to respond. "I…I know it's a serious matter. I told you when I first came to you that…that I was serious about finding a wife. And I'm ready. Ruby and me... Ruby and I," he corrected. "We've talked and we both want to court. Each other."

Sara raised an eyebrow speculatively. "Ruby told you that she's interested in courting you?"

"*Ya*, she did. She and I... We...we agreed."

Sara sat back in her chair. It was an oversize office chair, crafted of oak and comfortably cushioned. The chair swiveled and rocked. It was a chair that Joseph had seen at the chair shop and greatly admired, but it was big for a woman of Sara's size. She resembled a great-aunt of his, someone who'd always sneaked him cookies when he was a child. The thought of Aunt Rose made it feel a little easier talking to Sara.

Her smile widened. "Your mother said you were shy and that you had a difficult time expressing yourself. That doesn't seem to be the case at all. I'm impressed. And frankly, young men rarely impress me."

"I can support her... Support Ruby. And my mother. Mother has to live with us. But I told Ruby, and she's fine with it. As a mason...a master mason, I can always get work. I'm working with James now. His construction company, I mean. He says he's got plenty of work for me. And...and I have a house. In my own name."

Sara wrote something in her notebook. "It's good to know that you are financially solvent.

That you can take on the responsibility of a household as a husband and father, if God blesses you and your future wife with children."

"I will. I mean…I expect to." He could feel perspiration trickle down his back. He needed to hurry this along, otherwise he'd be late to the job site and James would be disappointed. He liked to start on time. But this had to be settled first with Sara. About Ruby. He'd lain awake half the night worrying. He couldn't do that again. He realized that Sara was saying something about a dowry and he jerked upright, giving her his attention again.

"Do you mind?" she said.

"M-mind what?"

"Financial wealth of a girl's father." She peered over her glasses at him. "Is that something that's important to you?"

"Ne." He shook his head. "I don't care. Money…money isn't important to me. I mean… it is, but I don't expect… It doesn't matter. Ruby could be penniless. It's fine." He took a breath. "So, are we courting? Officially?"

"Ne. You are not. Not yet. It's simply not the way I operate," Sara said firmly. "I'm happy that you're committed, but I've had a lot of experience with matching couples. Often young people form attractions, infatuations, if you will. But marriages, *good* marriages are not built on infat-

uation. There has to be more, things like mutual respect, compatibility and an equal commitment to faith. Think of it as laying a foundation." She indicated him with her hand. "You're a mason. You understand the need for a solid foundation."

"A house won't stand without it."

"Exactly. And for an Amish couple, the foundation is even more important. We marry for life. There's no divorce. Whoever you choose and whoever chooses you, chooses until death parts you."

"I—" A knock at the door interrupted what he was going to say.

"Ya?" Sara asked.

The office door opened and a man in a patched blue shirt and raggedy straw hat in his hand peered in. "Mule's thrown a shoe," he said. "What do you want me to do?"

"Take him to the smithy, Hiram. A mule can't work with three feet, can he?"

The door opened wider and Hiram stepped through. He was the man that Joseph had seen unloading a bag of feed from a wagon when he'd driven into Sara's yard. "Planning on cutting hay in that little field."

"Then it will have to wait. Tend to the mule first."

Hiram scratched his head. "Thought you'd say that."

"I'm in the middle of an appointment," Sara explained. "Close the door behind you."

"What do I do for money?" Hiram asked.

"The blacksmith will send me a bill." She raised a hand and waved at him. "Goodbye, Hiram. Thank you."

Hiram grimaced. "Leah said don't bother you. You got somebody in the office."

"That's right," Sara said. "When I'm with someone, I don't like interruptions unless it's important. *Extremely* important."

"But the mule threw a shoe," he said doggedly.

She smiled. Her tone was kind when she spoke. "And I trust you to take the mule to the smithy and have a new shoe put on."

Muttering to himself, Hiram backed out of the room and pulled the door shut behind him.

"My hired man," Sara explained. "I'm sorry. You were saying?"

Joseph stared at the toes of his work boots. "I was saying that I…that I think we're compatible. Very…compatible. Ruby, she…she's kind. She cares about people. I always wanted a kind wife, somebody who…would love me." The last three words came out as a whisper. It wasn't that the idea of love that embarrassed him, only saying it out loud. Because he *did* want a woman who would love him, someone he could love. Not just like. Once, when he was *rumspringa*, his running-around time before he'd been baptized, he'd seen a romantic movie at an *Englisher*'s house about a man and woman who were in love, and a message one of them had written and put in a bottle. The movie had been sad. It had made him tear up. But it had been a notion he'd remembered. He didn't think his mother and father had loved each other like that. Was it greedy to want it for himself?

"Marriage isn't just about a man and a woman," Sara was saying.

He wondered if she'd heard what he'd said. What he meant about wanting romantic love in his marriage.

"Marriage is about family," she continued. "Family and faith, respect and friendship."

"And love?" he asked, daring to repeat himself and reveal his inner hope.

"Sometimes a couple will be fortunate enough to find love ahead of the marriage, but usually it comes later. That said—" she held up her finger "—there's nothing wrong with searching for love. At least I don't think so. But to get back to you and Ruby, we have to go slowly."

He fiddled with the brim of his hat. "And what if we don't want that? Ruby and I?"

"I insist. Who is the expert here, Joseph? There's a lot to consider. In your case, one issue is your mother. What do you think she would say if you rushed into an arrangement and started talking about marriage to a girl you haven't even walked out with?"

"I don't suppose she'd like that." He looked down and then back at Sara. "But Mother wants me to marry. She's the one who told me to come to you. She said I'd never find someone on my own."

Sara got up and came around the desk to stand only a few feet from him. Hastily, he got to his feet again.

"I'm sure Magdalena wants the best for you," Sara said. "But it's never easy for a woman to welcome another woman into her home. To give up her son to a wife."

"She'll have to accept Ruby. I can deal with my *mam*." He shuffled his feet. "But what if we want to marry and *you* don't agree? Do you have to approve of the match?"

Sara straightened her shoulders. "I can tell you that I once stopped a wedding on the morning of the marriage. I told the bishop and the elders that the couple was not right for each other. They called off the wedding."

"What did the couple do? Were they unhappy with you?"

"They were. At the time. But a few months proved that I was right. I told you—I know what I'm doing. I don't make careless matches. I make marriages that are strong and loving, marriages that will only grow stronger through the years. Do this my way, Joseph, and you'll never regret it."

"I suppose you're right," he admitted. "But I really…like Ruby. And she likes me." He considered for a moment and then asked. "What happened to the couple? Did…did they ever marry?"

Sara chuckled. "They did, but not to each other. The man married his almost bride's older sister and the girl married his younger cousin. Both marriages that I arranged. And they have worked out beautifully. Between the four of them, they have nine children, and it's only been seven years."

He glanced longingly at the door. "So what happens next? With me and Ruby? About, you know…taking it slowly."

"We'll start with a simple supper. Tomorrow night. Be here at six thirty, and bring your appetite."

"*Mother* will want to meet her. Can I bring her?"

Sara shook her head firmly. "Too soon. I'll invite Magdalena when it's the right time." She glanced at the schoolhouse clock on the wall. "And now I suppose you want to get off to work." She opened the door. "Have a good day, Joseph. And don't be late for supper. I hate it when young men keep my girls waiting."

Gratefully, he hurried out. He hadn't gotten all he'd wanted, but neither had Sara rejected him. He wasn't going to worry. Sara would see how perfect he and Ruby were for each other. He was certain of it. He couldn't wait to see Ruby tomorrow night, and he couldn't wait to tell his mother that he'd found the girl he'd been waiting for.

School was a half day, so Ellie and Ruby were back at Sara's by twelve thirty. After the midday-meal dishes were cleared away and the kitchen spotless, the two young women went into the garden to pick tomatoes. Leah and Arlene had gone to Fifer's Orchard to pick apples and Sara was catching up on her sewing.

Despite spending the morning together at the schoolhouse, Ruby was still shy around Ellie. The little schoolteacher seemed nice, like someone Ruby would like to have as a friend. But Ruby had never known someone with dwarfism before and was afraid that her habit of saying whatever popped into her head might cause a problem. She feared she'd blurt out something offensive that would ruin their prospective friendship.

At school, it had been easy to concentrate on the children and forget worrying about saying or doing something awkward. Children always had a positive effect on Ruby. She adored them, and they seemed to respond well to her. If things had been different at home, maybe she would have liked to have been a teacher herself.

The best way to keep from putting her foot in her mouth was to keep it closed, but being quiet never came easy to Ruby. So before she knew it, a question slipped out. "Why aren't you married, Ellie?" She tried to stop herself but it was too late. There it was, bobbing between them as obviously inappropriate as a mule in a kitchen. "I'm sorry," she said quickly. "I didn't mean—"

Ellie responded with a peal of laughter. "You mean why hasn't Sara been able to find me a husband? My fault, entirely. I'm too picky. I've had two marriage proposals since I got here, and I turned them both down."

Ruby plucked a tomato from a plant and carefully placed the fat tomato into the basket. If you bruised them, tomatoes could go soft before you could get them canned, and that would be a waste. "You did? Were the boys awful?"

Ellie tossed a rotten tomato into the space between the rows. "*Ne*, they were very nice. And one was very handsome." She giggled. "He was the hardest to refuse because I really liked him."

"But you didn't want to marry him?"

"Nope. I'm not even sure I want to marry. Maybe I like being single." Ellie ducked down behind a big tomato plant and all Ruby could see were the leaves shaking. "Ha. Thought you were hiding, didn't you?" Ellie reappeared, brandishing a perfect tomato. "The heritage tomatoes are the hardest to pick because they're not always that red color that gives them away. But they are delicious."

"I know," Ruby agreed. "I love them. They have more taste than the commercial varieties." She stood to her full height and rubbed the small of her back. Picking tomatoes was hard work because of all the bending. "The boys you turned down," she said. "Joseph Brenneman wasn't one of them, was he?"

Ellie giggled again. "*Ne*, not Joseph. But he's cute, don't you think?"

"He is." Ruby blushed and busied herself in searching for ripe tomatoes. "Was it awkward? Saying no?" she ventured after a few minutes of picking. "Refusing a man's proposal?"

"Not particularly. Only one of them seemed to take it hard, but he's found someone else, so I couldn't have broken his heart." At this, they both laughed together. As they reached the end of the row, Ellie brushed the dirt off her skirt, glanced up at Ruby and sighed. "My current problem is with a certain blacksmith that I know Sara would like to fix me up with."

"You don't like him?" Ruby furrowed her brow. "Or you don't think he'd like you?"

Ellie shook her head. "It's more complicated than that." She lowered her voice and moved closer. "I know Sara means well, but he's *little*."

"Little?" Ruby asked.

"Like me," Ellie said, throwing up her hands. "A little person. Jakob obviously likes me. But he's a pest, always trying to wrangle an invitation to dinner or showing up at the schoolhouse with some excuse or another. He's even trying to get my friends to put in a good word for him."

"Is that a bad thing?"

Ellie picked a tomato up from the ground, examined it, and then threw it hard against a fence post. The rotten tomato burst, sending a red-winged blackbird skyward in a flurry of tomato bits. "I would never date someone just because he's little like me." She gave a little huff. "Right now, I don't even want to think about it. I'm happily independent. I don't want to marry anyone. I love teaching at Seven Poplars School. I'm having the best time of my life and I don't have to do a man's laundry. But if I *do* decide to marry, it will be because he's the one and I can't live without him. Does that make sense to you?"

"It does," Ruby agreed. She wondered if Ellie

might like this Jakob more than she let on or if it was smart to rule out a person just because of his height, but she didn't say so. For once, she was able to keep her mouth shut.

"How are you two doing?" Sara called from the garden gate. "Finding many ripe ones?"

"Lots," Ruby answered. "I need to start another basket. This one's full." She picked up the basket with the tomatoes she'd just picked, but when she turned to carry it down the row, she tripped. The basket tipped and half of them rolled out onto the dirt. "Sorry," she said, making haste to recover the fallen tomatoes.

"Let me help." Ellie began putting tomatoes back into the basket.

Ruby was mortified. "Sorry," she mumbled again.

"Don't worry." Smiling, Sara walked toward them. "We'll start another batch of canning tomorrow. It won't matter if some of them are bruised." She stopped and made eye contact with Ellie. "*Ach.* I forgot my soup on the stove. Ellie, would you mind running in and stirring it? Just turn off the flame."

"I can do it," Ruby offered.

"*Ne*, let Ellie go," Sara said.

"But I don't mind," Ruby said, eager to help.

Ellie looked to her. "What Sara is trying to say politely is that she needs to speak to you alone."

"Oh," Ruby declared.

"It's how it works when you live in a match-maker's house," Ellie explained. "Watch out, Ruby, she's about to have a serious conversation with you." She giggled. "And unless I'm mistaken, it has to do with a certain bricklayer named Joseph." As she walked out of the garden, Ellie called back over her shoulder. "Remember what I said about the laundry, Ruby. Don't make any hasty decisions."

Nervously, Ruby looked back at Sara. "You wanted to say something to me that you didn't want Ellie to hear?"

Sara turned over an empty five-eighths basket and sat on it. She smiled at Ruby. "No need to fret. What I have to tell you isn't bad news. *Ne*, not bad at all. You have an offer of marriage. Quickest ever, for me." She shook her head in disbelief and folded her arms. "So fast and easy that I might not feel right collecting a fee for it."

Excitement bubbled up inside Ruby. So Joseph really had spoken to Sara, just like he said he was going to. She didn't know whether to jump with joy or drop to the ground in shock. She'd had offers before, but none she was so eager for. "Joseph?"

Sara rolled her eyes. "Of course, Joseph.

What other available man has laid eyes on you since you arrived? Other than Hiram, and he doesn't count." She chuckled. "Well, he counts. He's a sweet enough man under all that laziness, but he's certainly no match for a young girl like you."

Ruby shivered with delight. A young girl. The matchmaker had called her a girl. Sara knew she was twenty-five but didn't consider her over-the-hill. It was probably pride that made her take pleasure in hearing it, but she did. "Joseph really wants to marry me?" she asked, still unable to believe her ears. "He wasn't joking?"

"Not a joke," Sara assured her. "And not a match, not yet. There's much we need to discuss. Your parents made it clear to me that I was not to share your circumstances with any possible prospect. Now that Joseph has made his intentions clear, how do you feel about that? I've never counseled a would-be bride to keep such a big secret from her might-be groom."

She exhaled softly and considered. "I've worried about that. But I gave my word to *Daddi* and *Mommi*. They didn't think it would be wise to tell and asked that I not say anything. But that was before—" She chewed hard on her lower lip. "I don't want to be dishonest with Joseph, but I promised them. I feel as though I have to keep my word. What do you think?"

"I agree that this is unusual, Ruby. Your father explained that he doesn't want you judged for your circumstances. I don't often condone misleading a suitor, but I understand your parents' concern."

"My father is a wise man. And I know both he and *Mommi* want what's best for me."

"Mmm, *ya*." Sara picked a potato bug off a tomato leaf and dropped it into the dirt. She squashed it with the heel of her foot. "Nasty things," she said. "I'll never understand why the Lord created them, unless it was to teach us something I haven't learned yet." She met Ruby's gaze. "You might as well know that I'm a woman who says what she thinks. And I have to tell you that the swiftness of Joseph's proposal worries me."

Ruby made a sound but was able to keep herself from interrupting.

"I'm sure he's sincere, but these matters usually go at a much gentler pace. I had intended to introduce you to someone else." Sara narrowed her gaze. "Are you certain you wouldn't like to meet him before we proceed with Joseph's suit?"

Ruby shook her head. "*Ne.* I think Joseph is wonderful, perfect even."

Sara pursed her lips. "A perfect man I have yet to meet, although my former husbands all had excellent qualities. I'd be of an easier mind if you and Joseph would just date one another before you consider a formal courtship."

"*Ne.*" Ruby sighed. "I've been to enough taffy pulls and barn frolics. I'm tired of *dating.* If Joseph is willing, I am too. I would love to have him court me."

"Courtship is a serious matter. You'll be strictly chaperoned and the community's eyes will be on you. When you go out with Joseph, you'll be in at a decent hour and you will not be alone with him in any private place. And there will be no physical shows of affection. Do you understand?"

"*Ya, ya,*" Ruby replied, feeling herself blush. "I understand. That's fine. So what happens next? When can I see him?"

"Well…" Sara sighed as if resigned, though still not totally in agreement. "Joseph is coming to share supper with us tomorrow night. We'll see how that goes. Fair enough?"

"Fair enough." Ruby grinned. Tomorrow night! How could she wait that long? What would she wear? What would she say to him?

She clasped her hands together. "I can't believe this is happening," she managed.

"Neither can I," Sara admitted, coming to her feet.

Chapter Four

It was close to six o'clock when Joseph got home from work that night. He'd been laying a line of blocks on a house foundation and wanted to use the last of the mixed cement so that it wouldn't go to waste. It had been a hot day and he wanted to shower before supper. "I'll be quick," he promised his mother as he cut through the kitchen. "I've got something exciting to tell you."

"Your clean clothes are in there," his mother said, waving in the direction of the bathroom. She was her usual neat and tidy self. She didn't appear to be a woman who'd done a day's work and prepared supper on a warm evening. Her *kapp* and apron were spotless, her complexion was smooth and without blemish, and her shoes were newly shined.

Hair slicked and dressed fit to sit at the table,

Joseph took his seat twenty minutes later. He was so excited to share his news that he could hardly keep from tapping the tabletop or bouncing his heel up and down, both of which always made his mother unhappy. She didn't scold him the way she had when he was younger anymore, but she had a way of expressing her displeasure without words.

"Aunt Milly stopped by today and left us a carrot salad," she said as she placed a platter of cold ham and cheese in front of him. "So hot today, I thought we'd eat light. But if you're really hungry, I can fry some chicken."

"Plenty here," Joseph said. Which was an understatement. Besides the lunch meat and carrot salad, there was a platter of deviled eggs, coleslaw, sliced onions and tomatoes, Kaiser rolls, homemade applesauce, peanut butter, raisin bread and three quarters of a chocolate pie. "Maybe we should invite the neighbors."

His mother's eyes lit up as she poured lemonade from a crockery pitcher and handed him a glass. He had a weakness for her lemonade. His mother always froze her ice cubes with fresh mint or bits of fruit in season.

Joseph wondered if Ruby was a good cook. He knew that young women often had much to learn in the kitchen, but he didn't care. If he could have her to wife, he would gladly eat cold cereal three times a day. Even if he had to fix it himself. Of course, they would all be living together, and his mother, an excellent housekeeper as well as cook, could teach Ruby whatever she didn't know yet. *"Mam,"* he began, unable to contain himself any longer. "This morning, I—"

She silenced him with a slender fingertip to her lips. "Grace," she reminded him gently. She bowed her head and closed her eyes. Joseph did the same, willing his thoughts of Ruby to recede during silent prayer. Before long, his thanks to God for the food before him led naturally into gratitude for finding Ruby. So intent was he on expressing his joy that such a gift could come to him that he lost track of time and was surprised when he heard his mother's voice.

"Joseph? Are you listening to a word I say?"

He opened his eyes. *"Ya."*

"Goot. I was saying that Milly's neighbor Pauline has a daughter."

"That's nice." He picked up his fork to reach for a slice of ham, then put the fork down without retrieving the meat. "So I stopped at Sara Yoder's house on the way to work this morning."

"Something wrong with the ham? Too fatty?" She got to her feet and picked up the platter. "Here, let me trim it. It's delicious. I had a slice at lunch. Did you want mustard on that or mayonnaise? I didn't put the mayonnaise on the table. You never want to leave it out when it's warm. But I can get it."

He took the plate of cheese and meat from her hand and set it back on the table. "Mustard is fine. Now, sit down with me. I want to tell you about my talk with the matchmaker."

"I'm glad you brought that up. That's what I want to tell you!" She raised a small hand. "No need to waste your hard-earned money on Sara's fee. Aunt Milly's neighbor Pauline has a daughter in Indiana. Widowed, with three children, all boys. And the word is she's looking for a new husband. Aunt Milly says she remembers the woman well, very pious, makes excellent *hasen pfeffer*. Heda's a few years older than you, but that's no problem." She slipped back into her chair." It's always good for a young man like you to have a more experienced wife to guide him."

He glanced at her. "What do you mean, *a man like me*?"

"Oh, Joseph, hush. I'm not criticizing you. But you and I are both aware that you've never been forward. And Heda is the exact opposite. She knows how to get things done. She's run a household for ten years. She's frugal and understands how to manage money. Aunt Milly said her last boy was born in three hours. Can you believe it? And Heda was on her feet in time to cook dinner. Doesn't she sound perfect for you? I think that between us, we could arrange for you to go out and meet her. I was thinking—"

Joseph had picked up his glass of lemonade and now set it down sharply. "Mother, will you please stop talking long enough for me to get in a word?"

She crossed her arms over her chest, looking peeved. But at least she was quiet.

"You wanted me to hire a matchmaker," he said, gentling his tone. "You told me that my best chance for finding a wife would be to let Sara Yoder find me someone. And you were so right, because she has!" He went on quickly, before she could interrupt him again. "I've met the most wonderful girl. And the best part? She likes me too. I'm so certain that she's right for me that I went to Sara's this morning and asked for permission to court her."

His mother popped out of her chair again. "Court her? How can you possibly court her? How many times have you seen this girl?" Clearly flustered, she looked frantically for the paper fan she always kept nearby. She found it on a chair and began fanning herself. "You can't court a stranger. I haven't even met her. That's not the way it's done." She shook her head. "What can Sara be thinking? I knew I should be the one to speak with her first."

"Mam," he said quietly. "We've been together twice, but…but I knew the minute I laid eyes on her. She's the girl for me, the one I've been waiting for. And when you meet her, you'll see it too. I know you'll—"

"It's not right." She fluttered her fan in front of her face. Two bright spots of color bloomed on his mother's pale cheeks. "I can't give my permission."

He decided not to bring up the fact that he didn't need her permission to court anyone. Instead, he said, "Just wait until you meet her. You're going to love her. She's smart and she's beautiful and…and she can talk about anything."

His mother whipped the fan back and forth faster. The red spots had spread so that her entire face had taken on a flush and beads of sweat formed at her temples. "You can't really be courting this girl. You must be mistaken, Joseph. I'm sure you mistook what the matchmaker said. Nothing happens this fast. It *shouldn't* happen this fast. Not without consulting me. And what kind of a girl would agree so quickly?" She began to pace behind her chair, fanning her face furiously. "I know what you need. It's not this upstart but a sound prospect like Heda. Did I tell you that she's well set up? Her husband had a nice little farm, and now that belongs to Heda. When she sells it to move here, it will bring a good sum."

"Mother, please, listen to me." It was all Joseph could do to keep from losing his patience. He hadn't expected this response. He'd been so certain that his mother would be glad to hear about Ruby. "I'm not marrying Heda King," he said.

"She's not Heda King any longer. I think her married name is Miller but I could find out. I could ask—"

"Mother, you aren't listening to me. I know Heda. Remember? She went to school with me. And not only is she five or six years older than me, but she's a shrew. She was unkind to all the younger children. And she used to tease me about not being able to speak in class. And she can't be too good with finances because she kept failing the seventh grade. She was terrible at multiplication."

"That was years ago." She waved her fan in his direction. "I'm sure she's changed. That's the trouble with you. You're not willing to give a suitable young woman a chance. I'm sure if you go out to Indiana and meet with Heda, you'd find her just the woman for you."

"Ne." He shook his head, reaching for his

lemonade again. "I'm not going to Indiana to meet Heda. No Heda."

"But Aunt Milly assures me she'll make a perfect wife for you."

He took a sip of lemonade. "No Heda," he repeated. "The girl that Sara introduced me to…" He chuckled. "The same girl that sent me to the hospital with a cracked head. We suit each other. I've spoken to Sara and she's invited me to have supper with them tomorrow night. We'll get to know each other better, and Sara will give us the okay to begin courting. Officially." He reached for the tray of meat and cheese. "Now, please don't upset yourself. I'm handling this."

His mother sighed heavily. Her eyes reddened, and for a few seconds he was afraid she would start crying.

She waved the fan back and forth, stirring the warm air. It was an old fan and had once been painted with the date and the words *Delaware State Fair*, but they had faded and peeled away. Now it read "ware air" in faint lettering. The bouquet of roses had also faded to a smear of pink-and-yellow coloring, but his mother would not part with the fan even though he'd offered to buy her a better one. "What time are we expected for supper?" she asked weakly.

Joseph shook his head, not looking up at her. "Not us, *Mam*. Me."

"That's ridiculous. No young man from a decent family starts courting a girl her family hasn't even met. If your father were alive, Sara Yoder wouldn't think of trying such a thing." She picked up her plate to carry it to the sink. She'd never put anything on it. "The proper thing would have been for Sara to invite me. And I won't hesitate to tell her so."

"I'm sure Sara will ask you to come soon, but tomorrow night, it's just me." He'd lost his own appetite, as well, but he had no intentions of allowing his mother to see that. He cut off a small piece of ham and picked it up with his fork. "Once the arrangements are settled, I'll invite my girl to come here and meet you." He put the meat into his mouth and forced himself to chew. It was tasty.

"I don't know anything about this young woman. Where is she from? Who is her family? Is it anyone I know?"

Joseph took a little of the tomatoes and onions. He'd make himself eat a little. After all, his mother had gone to the effort to prepare and serve the meal. "All I'm going to tell you is that she has a kind heart and she's from Lancaster County. I don't think you know her family."

"A stranger? Not even local? What church does she belong to? You have to be careful. You're baptized. You can't go around courting girls from liberal churches. What if she's too good for a horse and buggy and expects you to drive a car? They do, some of those Amish in Pennsylvania. Not Amish at all, if you ask me."

Joseph took a spoonful of the applesauce. He hadn't seen his mother get this worked up in a long time. But it didn't matter. No one, not even the matchmaker could persuade him that Ruby wasn't the one for him, the one he wanted to make his wife.

"I trust Sara not to introduce me to a young woman who isn't Old Order Amish."

"What's her name?" His mother's voice was softer now, coaxing. "You can at least tell me her name. I hope it isn't Swartzentruber. We have Swartzentrubers way back in the family on your father's side, and she could be related, a cousin even."

"Her name isn't Swartzentruber." He started to speak her name and then realized he didn't want to. Not yet. Because for the first time in his life, he felt as if he had something that was his and his alone. And he wasn't ready to share it. He wasn't ready to share Ruby with his mother.

She stopped the motion of her fan. "You won't tell me her name?"

"All in good time." The applesauce was sweet on his tongue. He could taste the spicy tang of cinnamon and just a hint of nutmeg. Delicious. He helped himself to more.

"Well, I never." His mother fanned herself again. "I'm hurt, Joseph. I have to be honest with you. I'm hurt."

"I'm sorry, *Mam*. I wouldn't hurt you for the world. I didn't plan for things to go this way. I didn't expect to meet her so quickly. But that's what's happened. Now, sit down with me and eat something."

"I couldn't possibly eat." His mother stood behind her chair, resting her hand on it. "A wife becomes part of the family. Marriage is all about family." She shook her head. "This isn't a good beginning for what should be a happy occasion."

"It will be a happy occasion, I promise you." He took another piece of ham. "You and my girl are going to love each other."

"We'll see about that, won't we?"

He took a Kaiser roll and began to make a sandwich.

"Well," she exclaimed, looking away. "I suppose this means that I'm not going to Sara Yoder's with you tomorrow night."

He grinned to himself. "*Ne*, Mother. You aren't."

"I won't be able to eat a bite," Ruby said to Ellie as she drew aside the curtain and peeked out the kitchen window to see Joseph talking with Hiram at the long picnic table under the trees. It was cooler today than the day before, so pleasant that Sara suggested they take advantage of the lovely weather and eat supper outside. "I'm as jumpy as a hen on ice. I'll do something silly, I know it. Either that or I'll say something silly. If he hasn't already come to tell Sara he's changed his mind, he will then."

"Ruby, Ruby, no need to get yourself in such a state," Ellie soothed. "We're just having supper together." Her blue eyes sparkled with amusement. "There's no reason to fret. If you don't say much, Joseph will just think you're shy."

Ruby grimaced. "He already knows better than that. I talked his ears off the other day." She pressed her hand to her midsection. "I think I feel sick. I might get sick."

Ellie laughed. "You're not going to get sick. You're going to help me carry out the rest of the supper, and you're going to enjoy our meal. You like Joseph, and he likes you. There's nothing to worry about. It will be fine."

"You can say that," Ruby replied, "but that doesn't make it true. You don't know me. I'm a klutz and I say whatever comes to mind. I can mess up anything."

The back door opened partially and Sara

popped her head in. "Girls, the men are getting hungry. Let's move this along."

"We'll be right out," Ellie called as she opened the refrigerator. "The ham's not sliced," she told Ruby when Sara was gone. "I think one of us was supposed to do it."

"I'll slice it and bring it out," Ruby said. "You carry the pickled beets. I might spill those on Sara or Joseph, and beets stain." The ham was heavy. She wasn't sure if Ellie could manage it, but didn't want to say that.

Ellie took the bowl of beets in one hand and the peppered cabbage in the other, and then used her hip to push open the screen door. "Ruby, don't look as if you're going to a funeral," she called back. "This will be fun."

"*Ya*, fun," Ruby agreed half-heartedly. She found a sharp knife and moved the ham from the refrigerator to the counter to cut it. At least Sara was serving ham and not fried chicken. Ruby had a vivid memory of once carrying a plate of fried chicken to the men's table at a barn raising. She hadn't done a thing wrong all day, and she'd been feeling quite sure of herself. "Here it comes!" she'd called to the bishop just before she'd tripped over a cat and sent the pieces of chicken flying—literally flying— through the air.

A thigh had landed on the bishop's head,

while a breast had knocked the visiting preacher's hat into the Jell-O salad. The cat had made off with a drumstick, and the rest had scattered on the ground. The only positive note had been the single wing that bounced onto the bishop's plate. He liked wings, he'd assured her, which made everyone laugh all the harder. Ruby's mother had tried to console her by reminding her that no one went away hungry. There was always plenty at a barn raising. But she'd never been able to live it down. And even her father had teased her about it whenever they were having chicken.

Ruby wished her mother were here now. Her *mommi* always knew how to put things into perspective. Ruby had attempted to write to her last night to tell her about Joseph and how much she liked him, but she couldn't find the right words. After three starts, she'd given up and dropped the torn-up sheets of paper in the trash. Maybe it would be better to wait a few days and see what happened, she reasoned. By tomorrow, Joseph might have realized what she was like and moved his attentions to another prospect. She didn't think he would though. And if things did go well tonight, she'd have more to tell her parents.

Ruby picked up the knife to start slicing and then hesitated, remembering all too well the flying pieces of chicken. Maybe it would be better to carry the ham out to the table and cut it up there? After a moment's hesitation, she picked up the platter and pasted a smile on her face. *Please, please*, she prayed silently. *Keep me from making a fool of myself in front of Joseph.*

Everyone was at the table, and as she crossed the lawn, their faces turned toward her: Hiram, Sara, Leah, Ellie and Joseph. Ruby walked slowly, carefully balancing the ham on the platter. *I won't stumble*, she told herself. *I absolutely won't—"Ach!"* she cried as the ham suddenly slid forward on the plate. Ruby stopped short, fighting to keep the plate level. The ham had slid across the plate like a hockey puck on the ice on her father's pond. She stood there, frozen, afraid to move.

"Need some help?" Joseph offered. He rose and strode toward her.

Gratefully she looked into his handsome face. *This can't be true*, she thought. *It has to be a dream. This wonderful man can't be asking to court me.* Joseph reached out for the platter, and somehow, in the exchange, Ruby tilted the right side and the slippery ham slid off and landed splat in the dirt.

Ruby stared at the ham on the ground. *"Ne,"* she groaned. "Not again."

"My fault," Joseph said. "I… I distracted

you." He was looking right at her. Right into her eyes.

Ruby shook her head.

"Not to worry," Sara said, appearing beside Ruby to scoop up the ham off the ground. "Come on, Ruby, let's just get the other one. It's already sliced."

"Should…should I…help?" Joseph took a step forward and Sara waved him back.

"*Ne, ne*, we cooks can tend to this. Sit down. We'll be right back. Ruby?" she called as she walked away, the big ham in her hands.

Mortified, Ruby followed Sara into the house. "I'm so sorry," she said, once they were inside. She clutched the empty plate. "I don't know how it happened." It was all she could do to hold back the tears welling up in her eyes. And the knife. She'd left the knife in the grass somewhere. What if someone stepped on it? What if it went right through Joseph's foot? He wouldn't want to court her if he had to go to the hospital a second time in one week on her account.

"It's not a problem," Sara said. "I did the exact same thing myself last Christmas. Now, just get a hold of yourself. Joseph Brenneman doesn't want to court you because you can serve at the table. What he *does* want is a smiling face. You have to laugh off the small things, Ruby. Life is too full of big things to worry yourself over the small." She turned to the sink. "Now, put down the plate and go change your apron while I wash the dirt off this ham so I can slice it."

"But I thought you said…" Ruby stared at her wide-eyed. "You don't have a second ham?"

"Don't I?" Sara chuckled as she patted the ham dry with a clean kitchen towel and set it on a cutting board on the counter. "Foolish of me. I must be getting forgetful in my dotage." Her dark eyes lit with mischief. "I won't tell if you don't. Now, you make yourself pretty while I slice up this *other* ham. Hurry, or your Joseph will starve to death before he ever gets the chance to propose to you."

Minutes later, Ruby and Sara were back at the table under the trees, silent grace had been shared and they were passing the old pewter platter of sliced ham around. Ruby thought it had been clever of Sara to change service dishes, but then, she was coming to realize that the matchmaker was a wise woman on so many levels.

Once the meal commenced, Joseph had little to say, but he ate plenty, and twice Ruby caught him smiling shyly at her. She smiled back, still uneasy after the ham incident, but with Ellie, Sara and Leah keeping up a lively chatter, Ruby began to relax.

"Have another biscuit," Ellie told Joseph. "They're light as air."

"Ya." He nodded and reached for another biscuit.

Ruby blushed with pleasure and looked down at her plate.

"Ruby made them," Sara proclaimed to everyone at the table. "Her grandmother's recipe. She won't tell us what makes them rise so."

"You'll have to give me some pointers," Leah said. "When I was in Brazil, we could rarely get baking powder that hadn't already expired. Some of my biscuits were more like crackers."

Sara rose and refilled Joseph's iced tea glass. "Our Leah will be marrying soon. She'll need that help or her new husband will be complaining that she's not the cook his mother was."

Leah and Ellie giggled. "Good thing he couldn't come for supper tonight," Leah teased. "From the taste of these biscuits, he might have dropped me and started courting Ruby."

"You couldn't possibly make biscuits as bad as my aunt Anna's," Ellie put it. "Hers were so hard that her kids wouldn't eat them. They would sneak them out to the chickens, but they were even too tough for the chickens."

Laughter and more lighthearted stories flowed across the table. Joseph took a third biscuit, buttered it and devoured every bite. Hiram ate doggedly, not speaking and rarely looking up from his plate. And before Ruby knew it, Leah and Ellie were bringing out the pies.

Soon the meal was over and Ruby began to worry that she'd cause another disaster clearing away the dishes. She rose and began to gather the plates, but Sara took them from her. "Plenty of hands to make this work light," she said. "You young ones need to go and sit and talk a little. Joseph, would you mind taking Ruby over to the gazebo?" She indicated the one in the side yard. Under the roof were porch swings, benches and chairs for relaxing. "You go on. I'll join you shortly."

Joseph flushed but got to his feet and looked expectantly to Ruby. "Will you come? W-with me?" he stammered.

"Oh, yes," she agreed. The gazebo was on the opposite side of the house from the fishpond and it was near the driveway. The sides were latticed wood, open enough so that a couple could be seen inside, but closed in enough so that there would be a feeling of privacy.

Shyly, she walked beside him across the yard. He stood back and let her step up into the gazebo. "Good…good supper," he managed as she took a seat on the nearest swing.

"Good ham," she said, and they both laughed.

"A second ham," Joseph said and laughed all

the harder. He sat down beside her and gave the swing a slight push. "And the—the best biscuits…I ever tasted."

As she looked up at him, Ruby sighed and all the worry seemed to slip away.

Chapter Five

Joseph looked at Ruby sitting beside him under the gazebo and his heart knocked against his ribs. It was pounding so loud that he was certain Ruby must hear it. He had so much he wanted to say to her, but as usual, he couldn't turn his thoughts into words. "Good…good supper," he squeaked out. Heat washed up his throat, burning his cheeks. It was all he could do to keep himself seated there in the swing beside her.

All of his insecurities chipped away at his confidence. Why would this wonderful woman choose him? He'd wanted to date other girls over the years. Not *date* exactly, but drive home from a singing or a frolic. Most of them had turned him down flat. Why should Ruby be any different? She'd told him she wanted to court him, true, but maybe she was simply too kind to hurt his feelings. Maybe that was why she'd

come out here with him. Maybe she was pre-
paring to tell him that it was all a mistake and
she didn't want to court him.

His hands were damp and he rubbed them
on his trousers. Beads of sweat trickled down
the back of his neck. He was going to ruin any
chance he had of having her for his own through
his confounded shyness. And then, he realized
that she was saying something.

"I was so embarrassed that I dropped the
ham," Ruby said. "I feel like such a silly—"

"Ne," he said abruptly, cutting her off. He
turned toward her and looked directly into her
large, beautiful eyes. "You shouldn't—shouldn't
worry about things like that."

"That's what Sara said."

"And she—she's right. The food was delicious. No one minded."

Ruby smiled at him. "Sara said she would get
the other ham. But there wasn't another one.
She washed the dirt off and we sliced the one I
dropped," she confided. "I wouldn't want you
to think that I was trying to trick you."

"Really?" He started to relax. "That was
smart of her."

"So you don't think it was wrong?" she asked.

He chuckled. "It's what my mother would do.
Maybe not say she had a second ham, but she'd
sure wash it off and serve it. It would be waste-

ful to just throw away good meat." He paused. "And who knows what goes on in restaurant kitchens?"

Ruby giggled. "Maybe the cooks play soccer with the hams."

"To make them tender," Joseph suggested. When Ruby laughed at the idea, he felt quite clever. And he began to feel a lot better about being here. "Ruby... I don't talk much," he admitted. "In front of people. Like at...supper. I hope...you don't care." He made himself look at her.

"*Ne.* Of course I don't care. I didn't even notice. I'm just the opposite." She chuckled. "You've probably already noticed. I open my mouth and I can't seem to stop talking."

"It's not that I don't think of stuff to say," he explained. "It—it just won't come out."

Ruby thought for a moment before she responded. "My father always says that it's better to be quiet and be thought wise than to open your mouth and prove to be a fool. I try to remember that, but I guess not often enough." She laughed, and Joseph found himself chuckling with her.

He sat up a little straighter. Ruby was easy to talk to. He liked being with her. No matter what happened, they ended up laughing together. He looked down at her and gathered his courage.

"I—I was afraid you'd had second thoughts. After you...you know, thought about it."

"About us?" She shook her head. "*Ne,* I haven't." She offered a shy smile. "But I was afraid you'd changed your mind."

"Not at all. In fact...I—I couldn't wait to come here tonight. To see you again." He exhaled slowly. Things were definitely looking up. He gave a small push with the toe of one shoe and the swing began to move. "I guess Sara told you, but I talked to her about—about you and me courting. I told her that we both wanted it."

"I did too."

"You did?" He looked down at her pretty face again. "So, are we? Courting? Each other?"

Ruby blushed and covered her face with her hands. "*Ya,*" she whispered. "I think we are." She lowered her hands and looked up at him. "If it suits you, Joseph."

Happiness bubbled up inside him. "It does," he answered. "It suits—suits me fine."

He was still looking into Ruby's eyes when he heard Sara coming across the lawn toward them.

"I don't hear any shouting, so I suppose you two are still getting along," she said as she entered the gazebo. Joseph leaped to his feet but she motioned him back with a quick wave of her hand. "Sit, sit." She perched on the arm of one of the wooden chairs and glanced from one to the other. "I take it you two have talked and that you both wish to proceed with this arrangement?"

"We do!" Ruby cried, clasping her hands. "We're perfect for each other."

"Ya," Joseph agreed. He removed his straw hat and held it tightly. "Perfect."

"So what's next?" Ruby asked. "Do we introduce each other to our families? We'll get to spend time together, right?" She glanced at him and back at the matchmaker. "Because we want to spend time together. As much as we can."

Again, Sara raised a hand. "I'll explain it all," she said. "You have to understand that these are unusual circumstances. Normally I ask, or rather, I allow my couples to get to know one another before entering any kind of formal agreement. If you're just riding home from singings together and such, there's a lot more privacy. Folks tend not to pay attention too closely to couples just dating. A young couple just dating, or maybe *rumspringa*, might be sneaking out of the house after dark to go for a buggy ride. It's only right that young men and women meet lots of people so that they can pick the one right for them. The community understands this, and the rules are loosened for this special time. That way, if the match doesn't work out, no one needs to feel any embarrassment."

Joseph exchanged smiles with Ruby. This was going smoother than he'd hoped.

"But with official courtship," Sara said, "it's very different. I need to be sure you two understand that courtship is serious. Couples who court think that they want to marry each other."

"We do," Ruby said, placing one hand very closely to his on the swing. "Don't we, Joseph?"

He nodded. "*Ya.* We—we do."

Sara fixed them with a cautionary gaze. "I just need you both to understand that courtship will be more restrictive than dating would be. When my couples are courting, I'm conservative, which means I expect you to have an escort when you go somewhere together."

"You mean, like a chaperone?" Ruby asked. "But at home in Lancaster County, courting couples are free to come and go as they please. As long as...you know, they behave themselves."

"Which is why I'm suggesting maybe you should just date for a few weeks, a few months."

Ruby met his gaze questioningly. "Do you just want to date? I don't want to just date, do you?"

Joseph swallowed hard, moving his gaze to Sara. "We don't want to... We don't need to date. We want to... We're ready to court."

Sara looked at them for a moment. "I just want to be sure this is what you want. This isn't a lighthearted game. Many young people fall into infatuation, sometimes more with the *idea* of marriage than with a particular person. None of us is perfect. You have to get to know each other so that you can decide if your partner's weaknesses are ones you can accept and love."

Joseph wanted to say that he already knew that any of her weaknesses didn't matter to him. Just like she said that his inability to talk in public didn't matter to her, but he couldn't quite bring up the words.

Sara turned to Ruby. "Are you certain you don't want to discuss this with your parents before agreeing to a formal courtship with Joseph?"

Ruby shook her head. "They trust me. I'm twenty-five, almost twenty-six. I know my own mind, and I can see what a good man Joseph is. They will be happy with him."

Sara glanced back at Joseph. "And you? You don't think you should take a little time to think on this?"

"Joseph knows his mind. He's older than I am." Ruby took a deep breath and rattled on about Joseph's qualities and maturity until Sara spoke up.

"I need to hear Joseph's opinion from his own mouth," the matchmaker said. "Are you certain, Joseph? This is your decision?"

"Ya." He nodded.

"And do you think your mother will approve of this haste?"

"My mother will be happy that—that I'm happy," he assured Sara with more enthusiasm than he felt. His mother could be difficult at times, and she was deeply attached to him. But once she realized how perfect Ruby was for him, she would welcome her into the family. Ruby would be the daughter his mother had always wanted.

He and Ruby reached for each other's hand at the same time. Her warm fingers closed around his, and a sweet sensation flowed up his arm. "Is—is it all right?" he asked Sara, looking over to her. "To hold hands?"

Sara grimaced. "Most of my couples wait more than a few minutes after declaring their wish to court before moving on to intimacies such as hand holding. And I'd strongly suggest that you two do the same."

Joseph let go of Ruby's hand and felt himself flush. He couldn't mess this up. He had to do this right, for Ruby's sake. Everyone must see what a great match they would make. And nothing could sully her name.

"So we're officially courting?"

"It appears that you are," Sara answered, getting to her feet.

Ruby squealed with delight and leaped up and threw her arms around Sara. The older woman almost lost her balance and Ruby had to grab her with both hands to keep her from tumbling back. But Ruby was still bouncing with excitement as she righted the matchmaker and hugged her. "Thank you, thank you," Ruby said breathlessly. "You're wonderful. And Joseph—Joseph is the—"

Ruby turned to him as he rose from the swing, and for a second he thought she was going to hug him, as well. Drawn by her vibrancy and caught up in the excitement, he opened his arms. But Sara's voice cut through their exuberance.

"Indeed not," Sara scolded. "There will be no embracing in my presence or out of it. You two will conduct yourselves properly. I do have a reputation to protect. And I've given my word to your parents, Ruby." She waggled her finger at him and Ruby. "So I'm warning you both, behave yourselves."

"Ya," Joseph agreed, tucking his arms behind him. He couldn't stop grinning. "We will."

"Absolutely," Ruby agreed, meeting his gaze again. "But it won't be easy."

Later that evening, when the house was quiet, Ruby removed the cap from her pen and began her letter to her parents in English.

September 5,
Seven Poplars, Delaware

Dearest *Mommi* and *Daddi*,
I pray that all is well on the farm and that
you both remain in good health. Everyone
here is nice to me. You would like Sara
Yoder, the matchmaker. As Aunt Ellen
would say, Sara has an old head on her
shoulders. I have already made a new
friend here at Sara's house. Her name is
Ellie, and she has blond hair and blue eyes
and is pretty. You would not guess what
is special about her besides that she is the
schoolteacher. Ellie has dwarfism but Sara
calls her a little person, and I think Ellie
likes that best. Ellie is such a happy and
busy person. We laugh together all the
time. She is a little older than me and has
a suitor, but she wants nothing to do with
him. I think maybe she protests too much
and likes him a little. Ellie is funny and
smart, and she can do anything I can do,
even though she's short. Usually better.
Certainly without dropping the ham. That
is a long story and I will tell you about it
when I see you, which I hope is soon because I miss you all so much.

Does Bretzel miss me? I miss him. I

keep looking for him to come around the corner, wagging his tail, or coming to curl up on my feet as he always does. Has Polly had her foal yet? I can't wait to see if it is a bay or piebald like the *fader*. Did you get rain? I hope the garden is still producing well. I'm sorry I'm not there to help with the canning. I remember my prayers as you told me, and I pray for you both every night.

I saved the best news for last. Sara has made a match for me. His name is Joseph and you will love him. He is a hardworking mason and is kind and sweet. He is also shy but doesn't mind that I am not or that I am a klutz. *Mommi*, I don't think he cares that I am plain even though he is not. *Ne, Daddi*, I will not say that Joseph is as handsome as you, even if I think it. I am so glad that you talked me into coming to Seven Poplars because I now have a beau who knows nothing about me. I feel bad not to tell him, but not so bad as to break my word to you. We will have to talk about when to tell him.

My heart is so full that it is hard to write my thoughts. I think I love Joseph and we are officially courting. I hope you will meet him soon. That's all I have to say. Tell Aunt

Ellen that I miss and love her. Remember me in your prayers.
Your obedient daughter,
Ruby

"This is Spence's Bazaar and Auction," Sara explained as she guided the mule and wagon through the crowded parking lot. "It started off years ago as a traditional livestock and farm produce market, but now we sell Amish and Mennonite food and vegetables, and there's a giant flea market that draws locals and tourists. They sell everything from furniture to hammers. Lots of people come, Amish and English."

Automobiles and trucks filled the haphazard rows, and throngs of people wandered between the vehicles, headed toward the buildings and stalls or back to their cars. "I don't imagine that you have any trouble mixing with the English, Ruby," Sara continued. "You have a lot of tourists in Lancaster. So you can help Arlene if she needs it."

Arlene, wide-eyed, nodded shyly. Her home was a small rural community in the Midwest, and she seemed a little awed by all the *Englishers.*

"Of course I will," Ruby said, taking in all the sights and sounds. "I think we have more traffic on the roads than here. Lots of buses from all over. In summer, if you go into Bird In Hand or Kutztown, it can be hectic. Tourists everywhere." It was Friday morning and she had come with Sara and Arlene to Spence's. Joseph had promised to meet her here, and she was excited to see him.

"You girls go on," Sara said as she found an open space in a row of buggies to hitch the mule. "I'll catch up with you. You'll find Leah at the far end. Her betrothed's vegetable stall is on the east side. The awning is blue and white."

"We'll find her," Ruby said.

Leah's sister Grace, who was Mennonite, had picked her up early that morning to drive her to Dover. Leah had a big family in Seven Poplars, and her husband-to-be was from the area, as well. Together, they were starting an organic-vegetable business with plans to supply restaurants and specialty markets. Leah had asked Ruby and Arlene to give her a hand today as her beau was busy in the field.

As Sara predicted, the two of them quickly located Leah. "Oh, good, you're here," Leah called in *Deitsch* when she saw them. "I'm swamped. Arlene, could you restock while Ruby helps me wait on customers?"

Ruby circled the table. She removed her black bonnet, put it and the spare apron she'd brought along in Leah's buggy and hurried to take a place beside Leah.

An English woman with a toddler in a stroller pointed at the potatoes Leah had placed in a wooden crate. "This is all grown without pesticides?" she asked.

"Absolutely," Leah assured her. "Everything on the table is grown organically."

"I'll take five pounds of the potatoes and a quart of those striped tomatoes," the woman said. "I have my own bag." She held up a green cloth sack that read Fresh Veggies.

Ruby smiled at her as she carefully packed the vegetables. "Thank you. Come again," she said when the woman paid her and tucked the produce into the bottom of the stroller.

As the customer walked away, a gray-haired man in a cowboy hat stepped forward to take her place and the line lengthened behind him. Ruby quickly learned the prices and soon felt more at ease as she, Leah and Arlene laughed and chatted between customers. Leah seemed to know everyone, and she introduced sisters, friends, aunts and cousins from the Seven Poplars community. Before Ruby knew it, more than an hour had passed and then another.

When the next lull in business came, Leah asked if they wanted anything to eat or drink.

"It's always busier as it gets closer to lunchtime, so you might want to grab a bite now."

"I'm expecting Joseph," Ruby said. "I told him that I would be here. We're having lunch together. But you go ahead. Arlene and I can manage until you get back."

"That works," Leah agreed. "I'll just grab something I can bring back here. Then you can go whenever you're hungry, Arlene. When Joseph comes, Ruby, take your time. Arlene and I will be fine."

Ruby wrinkled her nose. "Am I supposed to take Arlene with me? Sara was pretty adamant about me having a chaperone."

Leah chuckled. "I'm sure he'll bring his mother. I think Magdalena Brenneman will be chaperone enough to suit anyone. Be right back." She gave a wave and hurried away.

Ruby wondered about Leah's remark, but she didn't have long to think about it. Not five minutes later, she spied Joseph walking through the crowd. With him was a petite, slim, neatly dressed Amish woman, so youthful in appearance that at first, Ruby wasn't certain that she was his mother. The woman wore a dark blue dress, black apron, bonnet, shoes and stockings. She had light brown hair just like Joseph's. It framed her petite face, small straight nose and delicate chin.

Ruby waved wildly. "Joseph! Over here." Ruby was so excited that she could hardly keep from bouncing up and down. As she leaned forward on the table, she knocked into the bin of onions and tipped it. *"Ach!"* Some rolled over the front of the table, others rained around her feet.

Ruby ducked down to snatch the fallen onions just as Joseph reached the table and announced, "*Mother*, this—this is Arlene and this," he let out in a rush, "is my Ruby."

Ruby stood up and smiled at Joseph and Magdalena, her arms full of onions. She dropped one, grabbed for it and managed to drop two more.

"I'm so happy to finally meet you," his mother said to Arlene, clasping the young woman's hand in hers. "You're just a lovely girl."

Magdalena's voice was as sweet as her face, Ruby decided. It fit her perfectly.

"Joseph has talked of nothing else but you all week," Magdalena continued. "And I can see why. You're just perfect for him. Such a pretty girl."

Realizing Magdalena's mistake, Ruby looked from the older woman to Joseph's quickly reddening face and back to his mother again.

"Ne," Arlene protested. "I'm not—"

"And modest too!" Magdalena clapped her hands together. "My dear, we will get on—"

"Mother" Joseph protested. "That—that isn't…"

Arlene tried to back away from Magdalena. "You don't understand," she said. She was blushing too as she pointed. *"That's* Ruby."

"Ya, of course," Magdalena agreed. "That is Ruby." She nodded in Ruby's general direction. "Nice to meet you, Ruby." She returned her attention to Arlene. "But of course you're the one I'm here to meet, Arlene. I can't tell you how pleased I was when my Joseph told me he was courting." Apparently taking no notice of Joseph's distress, she beamed at him. "You've done very well, Joseph. I couldn't have picked a lovelier bride for you myself."

Arlene shook her head, her eyes now round with dismay. *"Ne.* Not me. I'm not—it's her." She pointed at Ruby and then turned sharply and made a beeline for the back of Leah's buggy.

"Mother, you…" Joseph insisted, clearly distraught. "You've…misunderstood. This—this is…*my*—my Ruby."

Magdalena's vivid blue eyes turned on Ruby. "You?" she said.

"Yes." Ruby let the last of the onions she'd picked up fall from her arms into the bin and stood as tall as she could. "Me. Ruby Plank.

I'm… Joseph and I are courting." She extended a hand, streaked with dirt and onion skins, across the table. "It's nice to meet you, Magdalena."

"Oh. I see." Magdalena's perfectly shaped mouth, her naturally pink lips firmed into a thin line as she returned a limp handshake. "Joseph said you were beautiful and I naturally assumed that…" She looked pointedly in the direction Arlene had fled.

Ruby withdrew her hand, dusted off the onion skins and folded her arms over her chest. Lifting her chin, she said, "If he said that, I can see how it would be an honest mistake to think Arlene was Joseph's bride-to-be." She cleared her throat and forced a chuckle. "I know what I am, Magdalena. I am as plain as a turnip. But Joseph doesn't seem to mind. And so neither do I." She met his mother's gaze with one she hoped was just as strong and just as determined. "And I am so pleased to meet you. Joseph speaks of you so highly."

"That's nice to know," Magdalena said tersely. She patted his arm. "There, there, Joseph. Breathe. You look as though you've swallowed a fishhook. There's no harm done. Had you told me her name as I asked, it would never have happened. And Ruby doesn't look to be the type to hold a grudge." She looked up at Ruby, meeting her eye to eye. "Are you, dear?"

Ruby stubbornly held the woman's gaze. "Of course not."

"Magdalena!" An Amish woman in a green dress waved to her from two stalls down. "Magdalena! This is the chowchow I've been raving about. Come and see."

"Coming," Joseph's mother answered. "I'll be right back. Don't go off without me, you two." Back straight as a fence post, black handbag on her elbow, Magdalena walked away without another word.

"I'm so, so sorry," Joseph said the moment his mother was out of hearing range. "She's right. That was all my fault."

Ruby shook her head. She'd had such high hopes that Joseph's mother would take to her at first sight. She'd hoped they'd become the best of friends at once, but she suspected that had been naive of her. And now some comments she'd heard from Leah and others who knew Magdalena made more sense. "Don't worry about it," she said softly.

"I should have warned you. I should have… we should have talked about this. *Mother*, she says whatever comes into her head. Sometimes, not as charitable as it should be. But…but her heart is in the right place. She's going to love you. I promise she will. She just takes…takes some getting used to."

Ruby swallowed back her hurt. "I've been accused of saying whatever comes into my head, as well," she admitted. "But I don't think she likes me."

"Nonsense," he protested. "She's just embarrassed over what happened."

"If you say so. You know her better than anyone." Ruby began picking up the onions and putting them back in the bin.

"Ruby, we haven't really talked about this but…but it's—it's important to me that you like her. That she… That she likes you. She means so much to me. She's a wonderful mother. You don't know how she's sacrificed, being a widow all these years. You've seen her. She could have married a lot of times, but she didn't. She didn't want me to have a stepfather that might not treat me well."

Ruby waited for him to look at her. "But what if she doesn't?"

He looked uncomfortable. "Doesn't what?"

"What if she doesn't like me, Joseph?" She picked up an onion she'd missed from the ground and tossed it to him. His hand darted out to catch it. "You said it's important that I like her. What if she doesn't like me?" she asked him. "Is it over between us?"

For a moment he seemed so taken by surprise by her words that he didn't respond. Then his words came in a rush. "*Ne*, don't say that. Why would you say that?" He gently put the onion back in the bin. "Doesn't the Bible tell us to respect our parents? To honor them?"

Ruby nodded. She knew she should just be quiet right now. She should let this subject go until a later time. Later, down the road when they knew each other better. But she couldn't just let it go. Joseph had to know how she felt. She looked up at him, hoping she wasn't making a terrible mistake by speaking her mind. "*Ya*, the Bible does say to honor our parents. But it also says that a man should put his wife first. Ahead of everyone." She rested her hands on her broad hips. "I'll do all I can to help Magdalena accept me. I'll give her the respect she deserves as your mother and as an older person. But if she doesn't give me the same respect, you may have to choose between us. Because I will never come into a household where I won't be welcome. Not even for you, Joseph."

Chapter Six

Ruby was still standing in front of Joseph, the produce table between them, when Leah returned with a can of soda and two slices of pizza. "Hi, Joseph," Leah greeted.

He mumbled a hello in her direction.

"I can take over for a while," Leah said. "It's not too busy inside right now. So go, have a nice lunch together."

"*Ya,*" Ruby agreed. "That would be nice. I'm getting hungry. You?" She smiled up at Joseph, sorry that she'd been so blunt about his mother. She didn't regret stating her position, but she didn't want to cause him any grief. Clearly, he was caught between the mother he loved and a growing affection he felt for Ruby, an affection that Ruby hoped might blossom into real love.

"I invited Mother to—to lunch," Joseph said. "If—if that's okay." His high cheekbones were dusted with a dusky red and Ruby could read the uncertainty in his eyes. She'd noticed that Joseph's shyness was more evident when others were present.

"Wonderful. We'll go find her." Ruby untied her work apron. "Let me get my good apron out of the buggy, and we'll go find her and ask her to join us."

Leah placed her pizza on the table and walked around to the other side. "There are picnic tables over there under the trees," She motioned toward a cluster of white tables not far away. "It's warm inside the restaurant area, even with the fans. You might want to get something and eat outside."

"Ya," Joseph agreed. "Outside is…good."

Ruby came around the table to Joseph's side. She smiled up at him. "Don't worry. I'm sure your mother and I just got off to an awkward start. Everything will be fine. I'm sure we'll become the best of friends."

He nodded, his features revealing both gratitude and wistful hope. Ruby's heart went out to him. He really was a very gentle man. In some ways, he reminded her of her father, although no one would ever accuse Solomon Plank of being shy. But they shared a genuine kindness.

"Looks like the picnic tables are filling up pretty quickly. Should I get us a seat?" Ruby asked.

"Sure, and I'll get mother," Joseph agreed.

Ruby found a good spot in the shade and Joseph and Magdalena soon joined her. "I'll get our lunch and you two can sit," Joseph said, clearly feeling awkward. "What would you like, Ruby?"

"I'd like a hot dog and water," Magdalena said, opening her small black purse. "Get us all hot dogs, the nice beef ones from the stand just inside the door."

She pulled out a ten-dollar bill and held it out to her son.

Joseph flushed and lowered his gaze to his boots. "I have money," he said under his breath.

"Ne, ne," his mother insisted, shaking the bill. "I won't let you spend all your hard-earned paycheck on me." She smiled up at him. "You know you have to count every penny. No one ever pays you what you're worth."

Joseph shook his head again, and Magdalena tried to push the money into his hand. He stepped back.

"You see what I have to put up with," Magdalena said over her shoulder to Ruby. "He's stubborn, just like his father." She turned back to him. "Fine. Have it your way, Joseph. But I'd feel better if you'd at least let me buy my own lunch. Then you'll just have to pay for yours and Ruthie's. We want mustard and relish on the hot dogs. No onion."

"R-Ruby, Mother." Joseph's tone was sheepish. "Her name is… It's *Ruby*."

If Ruby didn't know better, she would think Magdalena had purposely called her by the wrong name. "Ruby," she repeated, hoping her smile looked more genuine than it felt.

"Oh, I'm sorry. Of course. Ruby." Magdalena chuckled. "And your last name, dear?"

"Plank." Ruby looked to Joseph. "A hot dog would be fine, but I like mine with onion and ketchup. No mustard, please."

Magdalena chuckled, glancing at Ruby. "Onion? Didn't your mother ever tell you that a girl with onion on her breath will never catch a beau?"

"Ketchup and onion," Ruby repeated, thinking that if Joseph really wanted to marry her, he might as well know now that she liked onions. "And water will be fine for me, Joseph."

Magdalena held out the ten-dollar bill once more, but Joseph walked away, leaving Magdalena to join Ruby on the picnic table bench.

"Well, well." Magdalena set her purse on the table and sat down beside Ruby. "Isn't this a nice opportunity for us to get to know each other?"

Ruby could hear insincerity in the woman's

voice. But she truly *did* want to be friends with Magdalena, so she forged ahead. "I've been wanting to meet you. And…well, I just want to tell you that I know this must be difficult for you. Joseph and me courting. He told me that you're very close. I wouldn't want you to think that I'd ever try to come between a mother and her son."

"Never crossed my mind." Magdalena smoothed an invisible wrinkle in her skirt. "Because that would be impossible. Joseph and I share a special…" She sighed. "It's difficult to explain to someone who hasn't had children. But a son, especially a first and only, is very dear to his mother." She patted the bench between them. "Come closer, dear. Let me see the stitching on your dress and apron. It's very well-done. You must be an accomplished seamstress."

Ruby slid over and turned over the hem of her black apron so that Magdalena could inspect the tiny, neat stitches. "My mother made my dress and apron," she admitted sheepishly. The fact that she wasn't much with a needle and thread or a sewing machine didn't usually bother her, but having to admit it to her mother-in-law-to-be was a little daunting.

"Oh." Magdalena put a forefinger to her lips. "You have hook-and-eye fastenings on your dress, don't you? We don't see much of that.

Hooks and eyes, buttons, zippers on women's dresses." She indicated her own dress. "We use straight pins."

Ruby started to assure Magdalena there were no buttons nor zippers on her clothing, but the older woman went right on talking.

"Of course, our church communities are quite conservative. Probably more so than…" Magdalena frowned, her forehead wrinkling. "Where is it you come from, my dear? Out west?" She opened her black bag, removed a folded fan, opened it and began to fan herself.

Ruby bit down on her lower lip, then winced. This first meeting with Magdalena wasn't going at all the way she'd imagined it would. Ruby had gone over and over this meeting in her head, planning what she would say. What they would talk about. Showing Magdalena the best of herself and setting her at ease, letting her know what a good wife she would make for Joseph. It had never occurred to her that Magdalena might not like her. Or might not be all that likable herself. Joseph had said his mother would live with them after they were married and suddenly she was worried. Was that even going to be possible?

"Iowa?" Magdalena asked pointedly. "Wisconsin?"

"Pennsylvania." Ruby forced another smile. "Lancaster County."

"Ach," Magdalena exclaimed. "No wonder. You *Pennsylvania Dutch* are quite liberal, aren't you? Lancaster County, you say? I'm sure we have a few mutual acquaintances."

Ruby certainly hoped not. Someone who knew Ruby might inadvertently tell things that Ruby's parents didn't want told. At least not yet. Suddenly Ruby wished fervently that she'd never agreed to her parents' plan. She didn't like keeping secrets. Not even from someone as ungracious as Magdalena. But she couldn't think about that now. And she couldn't allow Joseph's mother to put her on the defensive. She was supposed to make the woman like her, so that she would give her approval of the wedding.

"Where in Lancaster County?" Magdalena nudged. "Exactly?"

"Oh…out in the country. Nowhere that you'd know, I'm sure," Ruby said. "A little town called Bee Bonnet. It's really not much more than a crossroad."

"Bee Bonnet? How quaint." Magdalena's eyes narrowed. She stared. "Have you joined the church?"

"I—I have," Ruby assured her, taken aback by the sudden change in the conversation. "When I was eighteen. Just like Joseph," she added.

Magdalena frowned. "Your father isn't one

of the automobile-driving Pennsylvania Amish, is he?"

Ruby chuckled, imagining her father driving a car. "*Ne.* A horse and buggy."

"Rubber tires?"

Ruby shook her head, fighting the urge to laugh. "Just like Sara's. Only, our buggy is gray instead of black."

"Magdalena!" a man called.

Ruby looked up to see an Amish man carrying a cardboard box crossing the street toward them. "Magdalena, I was hoping to see you here today," he called cheerfully in *Deitsch.*

Magdalena smiled and waved and then said to Ruby, "Elmer Raber. A lovely man. He has a butcher shop. You may have seen his stand inside."

Elmer was a short, solid man in his early fifties. He had a medium-length, curly beard that might have originally been auburn but now was a dull rust color. He was dressed in a black coat, blue shirt, black trousers and suspenders. "Magdalena," he repeated, a little out of breath. He nodded to Ruby. "Afternoon."

"Elmer, this is Ruthie Plank."

"Ruby," Ruby corrected. "*Ruby* Plank."

Magdalena covered her mouth and chuckled. "Did I say Ruthie again? Forgive me. Just a slip of the tongue. Elmer is a widower." She nodded in his direction and then her eyes suddenly widened. "Elmer's a widower," she said again. "And would be a fine catch for any single woman." She popped up off the bench. "Elmer, you should join us for lunch. My Joseph will be right back. Have you had your lunch? We were just about to have a bite."

"Already ate. I can't stay long, have to get back inside. Lots of customers today. Abe is a fine young man, but the stall runs smoother when I'm there. Just went back to the wagon to get more paper bags." He indicated the cardboard box under his arm. "People have questions about the cuts of beef." He smiled at Magdalena, and Ruby noticed one discolored front tooth in an otherwise pleasant, bespectacled face.

"Ruby is staying with Sara Yoder," Magdalena explained, sitting down again. "She's come to Delaware to find a husband." She patted Ruby's hand. "Don't be embarrassed, dear. Nothing wrong with it. I urged my Joseph to ask for Sara's help. She has great success with making matches."

"Good ones, so I hear," Elmer said.

"And I'm sure Ruby won't be looking long. She's a fabulous cook, and she sews beautifully. Such a delicate young woman. She'll make someone a wonderful wife." Magdalena looked to Ruby. "Elmer's a widower. I mentioned that, didn't I? Two years now, isn't it, Elmer? So sad to lose a life companion. But he has the blessing of children to fill his home."

"Not quite," Elmer said. "Blessings, true. Two sons and a daughter. But they're all grown, married and out of the house. I'm on my own, and I can tell you, I don't like it much." He looked to Magdalena again. "A house isn't a home without a woman."

"Joseph and I—" Ruby began, but Magdalena cut her off.

"Here he comes with our hot dogs." Magdalena popped off the bench again. "Joseph, Elmer Raber's here. You remember him." She flashed Elmer a smile. "I should get Joseph to stop by your stall and get a nice roast for Saturday dinner. You pick me out a good one, Elmer. Something about three or four pounds with just a smidgen of fat in it."

"I have just the thing for you, Magdalena," Elmer promised, smiling down at her. "Angus beef. The best. Aged to perfection. And maybe I'll tuck a pound of scrapple in with it. Just for you."

"Good to see you, Elmer," Joseph handed Ruby a hot dog. "Did you meet Ruby?"

"We're walking out together. Joseph and I," Ruby explained, glad to clear up any notion Magdalena might had given Elmer that she might still be looking for a beau.

"Well, not quite," Magdalena amended. Then she laughed. "You know young people today, Elmer. Always in such a hurry. But I've advised my Joseph to go slow. Marriage is for a lifetime. It's important to pick the right person."

"And to know her when you see her," Elmer said, grinning, his gaze on Magdalena again.

"Ya," Joseph agreed as he set his mother's hot dog down in front of her.

"You really should join us for lunch, Elmer," Magdalena told the butcher. "Joseph can run and get another hot dog."

"Like to." He shifted the box from one arm to the other. "But I better get back to work. Might have time for a soda after the lunch rush though. If you'll still be here, Magdalena. Good weather to sit outside here and chat."

"And a perfect day for—for Mother and my Ruby to get to know each other," Joseph said awkwardly.

"Magdalena is a fine woman." Elmer grinned at Joseph's mother. "I know you'll like her, Ruby. Everyone speaks so highly of her."

Again Ruby opened her mouth to say something, but wasn't quick enough.

"Don't," Magdalena protested. "You'll make me proud." She fluttered her fan and looked down at her plate. "Such things to say to an old woman."

"Not so old." Elmer winked. "You know what they say. A new broom sweeps clean, but the old broom knows all the hiding places. For the dirt," he added, and then chuckled at his own joke.

Just then, Sara walked up to the table. "There you are, Ruby." She set her shopping bag on the bench. "Afternoon, Magdalena, Joseph, Elmer." Her gaze met Ruby's and she smiled. "How nice to find you all having such a lovely time."

It was all Ruby could do to look down, bite her tongue and not say what she was really feeling.

"That's just what I was thinking!" Ruby exclaimed, turning on the stepladder.

"Whoa!" Joseph shot out his hand and caught the tipping paint can inches from the floor.

"Oops." She grimaced. Then they both laughed.

It was a Wednesday afternoon and she and Joseph had come to a work frolic for young couples organized by Leah's sister Miriam and her husband, Charley. Eight couples, including the sponsors, had gathered at the Seven Poplar Schoolhouse to paint the interior of the building and have a picnic outside afterward. Arlene and Leah were there as well as several girls Ruby hadn't met yet. Everyone seemed friendly, and conversation and laughter filled the schoolroom.

Since Joseph had promised to have her home before dark and they were riding in Joseph's wagon in full public view, Sara had allowed them to ride the short distance to the school unchaperoned. It was the first time they'd been alone together since Joseph had found her drying her hair beside Sara's fishpond, and Ruby had been enjoying every moment.

"Sorry," Ruby told Joseph. The paintbrush in her hand was dripping white paint down her arm.

"I'd better take that." He reached for the paintbrush. "Why don't I finish up this window trim?"

"Good idea." Ruby looked down at the spots of paint on her dress and stockings. "I warned you," she told him. "I'm prone to accidents."

"Ne." He shook his head. "Painting trim is tricky." He took her hand and steadied her as she descended the stepladder.

A thrill shot through Ruby. Had he held her hand a fraction of a second longer than was necessary? His touch was warm and strong, exactly like the personality that radiated from his bright blue eyes. "Not for Leah or Arlene," Ruby said looking at the two of them working on the opposite side of the schoolhouse. "They don't make a mess when they paint."

He smiled down at her. "Maybe not so much. But I don't mind." He released her hand and stepped back, but his gaze remained locked with hers.

How handsome he was in his short-sleeved blue shirt and dark trousers, Ruby thought. She wondered what he would look like with a beard. He'd always been clean-shaven when she'd been with him. But, of course, that would change if they married. *When* they married, she told herself. Nothing was going to go wrong with this courtship. She wasn't going to let Magdalena get in the way, or anything else. No matter what, she'd find a way to smooth the small wrinkles in their relationship. That was her job, wasn't it? As a woman, she would be expected to be the one to adjust, to bend to her husband's will. That's what the preachers said.

"I was happy that you came to church with me, Sunday," Joseph said as he swept the small brush over the trim in smooth strokes to even up her painting.

"*Ya*, I enjoyed your bishop's sermon. He seems like a down-to-earth kind of bishop."

"He is," Joseph agreed. "Easy to talk to. In fact, I got a chance to talk to him about an idea I've had for a while. About a new kind of windmill," he explained, moving along the window with his brush. "The kind *Englishers* are putting up. No Amish around here have one, but the bishop said he didn't see why it would conflict with our values. He promised to take it up with the elders at their next meeting."

"Wonderful," she said, beaming. She liked that they had plenty to talk about. That Joseph felt comfortable telling her things. It was funny how he seemed to have no trouble getting his words out, without stuttering or stammering, when they were alone.

"And Mother said lots of people asked about you," he added. "I hope you had a good time."

"I did." Ruby perched on the corner of the big teacher's desk. She noticed that it wasn't nearly as high as most desks and remembered that Ellie had explained it had been built to fit her small stature. "Everyone was so nice and welcoming. I like your friends."

"And they like you."

Around them, the other couples were also painting or scrubbing and polishing the paneled wainscoting. They were using latex paint so that it would be dry by morning. It was amazing how much could be done when there were a dozen willing hands. One of the men, a bearded widower named Joel began singing a fast hymn and soon everyone joined in. Ruby, who knew she had a tendency to get carried away and sing too loudly, kept her voice low so that her spontaneity wouldn't embarrass Joseph. His voice was rich and sweet, and Ruby was delighted to discover this talent of his.

"What did you think of Elmer?" Joseph asked when they'd sung the lively spiritual through twice and the schoolroom had become quiet again, except for the conversations of the various couples.

"Elmer?" She had to think for a moment to realize who he was talking about. "You mean your mother's friend we met at Spence's?"

"*Ya.* Mother told me she was thinking of inviting him to supper one evening. I think he likes her."

"I think he does too," Ruby agreed, with a giggle. "But I'm not sure that your mother realizes it."

"She must. She speaks so well of him. She went on and on about what a good husband he would make."

"Did she?" Ruby laughed, recalling how Magdalena had been extolling his virtues when she introduced them.

"Girls," Miriam called from the doorway. "It looks like we're almost finished in here. Could you come out and help me set up the food?"

It was amazing to Ruby how much Miriam

resembled her sister Leah. Miriam's face was a little rounder and her hair a darker auburn, but like Leah, she looked younger than she was. Ruby liked her, and she liked Miriam's husband, Charley, as well. Both of them went out of their way to include everyone and make the event fun.

"Ya," Arlene said. "We're coming."

"We'll be right there," Ruby replied.

"I'll be finished in two minutes." Joseph turned his attention from painting to Ruby. "Mother sent a dozen poppy-seed rolls and a jug of cider for the picnic. I'll have to run and get them. They're in the split-oak basket in the back of the wagon."

"That was kind of her." Ruby stood up from her perch on the desk. "We'll have plenty, I'm sure."

Every girl had brought food, which they'd combine and share, potluck-style. Sara and Ellie had prepared fried chicken and apple fritters. Ruby, who knew she would have burned them both had her hand been in the pot, had contented herself with packing the basket and making certain there were enough utensils and napkins to share. She wasn't ready to chance her cooking skills on Joseph or any of the other hapless couples.

Ruby glanced up at Joseph. "See you soon?"

"I'm right behind you." The way he looked at her made her face flush and she hurried for the door.

"What do you think of Joel?" Arlene whispered to Ruby as they walked out of the classroom. The other couples had filed out, leaving only Joel and Joseph still in the schoolroom.

"He seems nice," Ruby said.

"He is. Widower. He has an adorable little boy. I met his son today." She caught Ruby's arm and the two lingered for a moment in the addition that served as both a storage room and cloakroom for the small school. "I met Joel's mother too. Very sweet and welcoming."

"That's a good sign," Ruby whispered. "I don't think he would have introduced you to his child and family if he wasn't interested in you."

"That's what Sara says." Arlene beamed. "She's introduced me to two others, but I like Joel the best."

They exited the outer door and walked down the steps single file. Along the side fence line of the schoolyard were an assortment of horses and buggies. Ruby and Joseph were the only ones who'd come in a wagon. But there was a buggy that hadn't been there earlier. Oddly, the horse was hitched to the back of Joseph's wagon.

"What's *my mother* doing here?" Joseph asked, coming up behind Ruby.

She looked back over her shoulder. Joseph and Joel were walking side by side. Joel nodded to her and strode to catch up with Arlene.

Ruby fell back to walk with Joseph. "Your mother?" Ruby said. "I didn't know she was coming."

Joseph was frowning. "I didn't either. I hope nothing's wrong at home."

When they rounded the schoolhouse, Ruby saw that Magdalena was standing beside Miriam, talking and pouring lemonade at the long serving table.

"She seems fine," Ruby whispered.

"There you are, Joseph," Magdalena called, waving. "You'd better hurry. I'm not sure there's enough chicken."

"Mother," Joseph said quietly, as they approached the buffet table. "What are you doing here?"

"I realized that I'd made two pies for the frolic and had forgotten to remind you to put them in the wagon. I thought the best thing to do was to bring them myself and see if Miriam could use my help." She looked to Miriam, who was busy removing foil from covered dishes.

"Always glad of another pair of hands at a frolic," Miriam said cheerfully.

Charley, standing beside his wife, grinned mischievously. "Oh, *ya*. Especially a mother."

Miriam elbowed him, but Magdalena didn't seem to notice.

"Men, find a seat for you and your date on the blankets spread around the yard," Charley announced. "Each couple gets their own spot. I'll come around with drinks. The women will make up plates for the men's suppers, and all of us fellows will do the cleaning up after dessert. How does that sound?"

"Goot," Joel called.

The other men joined in with a chorus of *"ya"* and "sounds good."

"And don't eat too much," Miriam reminded them. "Because we're playing softball afterward, and it's men against the women."

"Are you pitching, Miriam?" a boy Ruby didn't know called out.

"She sure is," Charley said. "So watch out for her fastball."

"Do you play softball?" Joseph asked Ruby. Ruby nodded.

"Good. Because I love it. I catch," he said. "What position do you play?"

"First base," she answered. "But I don't mind outfield."

"Can you hit?"

She chuckled. "Just wait and see."

"Where would you like to sit?" he asked.

"You pick," she told him. "I'm getting the food."

Ruby watched Joseph walk across the lawn to a multicolored quilt spread out near the swings, and then she got in line with the other young women at the serving table. For a light supper, there were more choices than could possibly fit on one plate. She wondered what Joseph liked, then decided to choose what she liked and hope for the best.

A few minutes later, walking carefully and balancing several of his mother's poppy-seed rolls on top of the plate, Ruby joined Joseph at the quilt where he was sitting. "I wasn't sure what you'd want," she said as she held out the plate.

"Ach," came a familiar voice from behind her. "Joseph, I picked out your very favorites." Magdalena nudged Ruby aside with her hip. "Joseph can be particular about his likes and dislikes," she said sweetly. "I'm afraid I've spoiled him."

Blushing, Joseph got to his feet. "*Mother*, Ruby already—already...I have a plate."

"Nonsense," Magdalena said. "You can just give that plate to her. I've brought—"

"Your plate looks wonderful," Ruby said to Magdalena as she pushed the plate in her hands into his. "And Joseph can eat every bite just as soon as he finishes what I've picked out for him." She smiled up at Joseph. "You *did* say you were hungry," she teased.

He nodded, looking obviously uncomfortable. "I—I did."

"Good. See, Magdalena—" Ruby turned to his mother "—now I won't have to go back for seconds for Joseph. Now, if you'll excuse me, I'm going for my own supper." She smiled sweetly. "If you like, Magdalena, I can bring you one, as well."

Magdalena stood there, holding the plate of food. Her mouth opened but nothing came out.

"No?" Ruby said, still smiling. "Well, I'm starved." And with that, she headed back to the serving table, leaving Joseph to deal with his mother.

Chapter Seven

Andy Troyer pumped the handle and cool water gushed out of the spout behind Joseph's house. Andy removed his hat and thrust his head under the flow, letting the icy well water wash away the sweat and grime from his head and neck. He stepped back, sputtering, shook his shaggy, blond head and clamped his straw hat back on. "Whew, that feels better." Water streamed down his shirt and dripped into the dust around him, and a few chickens ran over to investigate and stirred up the ground with their scratching.

Joseph laughed and patted his cousin's generous midsection. "You're getting soft," he observed. "Maybe you're eating a little too much of your mother's pie. Pitching a little hay into the loft too much for you?"

"*Ne,*" Andy protested, patting his own belly. "This isn't fat. It's muscle." He adjusted a faded, black suspender and eyed the barn loft they'd just come from. "Heavy bales, them. And it's a warm day for late September. Been a hot summer too."

Joseph stepped up to the pump and drew a cupful of water. He drank it down, wiped his mouth and then pumped more. The well was deeper than most Delaware farm wells and it had always produced sweet, clear water without the hint of sulfur that sullied some sources. "I appreciate your coming over to help me get the hay in the barn. It's starting to cloud up in the west. I was afraid that we'd get rain before I could get it all under cover."

"Good timothy hay like this, I can see why you'd worry. I heard thunder a while back. A storm's heading this way, for sure. Maybe a little rain will ease this late heat wave." Andy removed his hat again and slicked his damp hair back. "Violet asked me to check with you. You'll be there for the wedding? To help out with setting up tables and such?"

Andy's sister was marrying in late October. Her fiancé was from Ohio but the wedding would be held at her parents' house.

"I sure will. Wouldn't miss it. I'll take the whole day off."

"Good. Violet is afraid to leave the setup for the midday meal in my hands." He chuckled. "I guess she doesn't think I know how to set up for a wedding."

"Well, tell her I'll be there. And…" Joseph hesitated. "Looks like I'll be bringing someone along. If that's all right."

"All right? It's better than all right." Andy playfully clamped his hand around Joseph's arm. "When am I going to get to meet this girl of yours?"

"Ruby?" Joseph smiled. "Soon enough."

"Whirlwind romance, so your mother told mine."

Joseph didn't respond.

"*Mam* says you haven't known Ruby long enough to be getting so serious," Andy went on. "She had some ditty about a marriage in haste."

Andy's mother was a sister of Joseph's father, and she'd always been a favorite aunt of Joseph's. He had no doubt that Aunt Frieda had his best interests at heart, but he was certain she'd change her mind about him and Ruby once she saw how wonderful she was.

"The time you've known someone doesn't always matter. It's like we've always known each other."

Andy sighed. "As much as I hate to do it, I have to agree with my mother and yours. My advice is to go slow, cousin. Marriage is for a long time. And you don't want it to be with the wrong woman." He leaned against the hitching rail and wiped his face with his blue-and-white handkerchief.

Joseph chuckled and pointed at Andy. "I think you're making it worse. You've smeared something black across your forehead."

"Figures." Andy took another swipe at his forehead with the handkerchief. "Look, I'm not trying to put my nose in your business. Knowing Aunt Magdalena, I imagine you have enough of that already. I'm just looking out for your own good." Andy motioned to the cup that dangled from a string, and Joseph pumped a cup of water for him. Andy drank it slowly and then went on. "Seriously, Joseph. You can't know Ruby that well in what? Two weeks since she's been here? How do you even know if you really like her?"

"Almost four weeks," Joseph defended, though it was closer to three. "Almost a month. But I do like her. A lot. I—I think I love her. I love her enough to ask her to be my wife," he added with a firm nod.

Andy gave a low whistle. "My *mam* says your mother isn't happy about that. Not that she doesn't like the girl, but your mother is concerned about the rush. Especially since Ruby is from somewhere else and no one knows the family. No one knows Ruby. She's a newcomer.

Mam says your mother's afraid Ruby might not be all she pretends to be." He scuffed the ground with his boot and looked up. "And I understand her point."

Joseph frowned. "A lot of advice from another single fellow. I don't see you finding anybody you want to spend the rest of your life with yet."

"True words." Andy chuckled. "But you don't have to be a farrier to know a driving horse goes better with four shoes than three."

"Besides," Joseph said, not sure he liked the idea of having to defend Ruby to Andy. Andy was his best friend. He didn't think it ought to be like this between best friends. "Ruby hasn't pretended to be anything. She's…she's…" He could feel exasperation growing in his chest. He never had trouble speaking his mind to Andy. They'd been friends since they were babies. They'd been together through school and all the church affairs and family get-togethers so long as he could remember. He'd been planning to ask Andy to be part of the wedding.

"Come on, I'm not picking on you. Or your girl," Andy said. "Just telling you what's on my mind. Now tell me what it's like, courting? Picking someone that you like better than all the rest?"

That was an easier question to answer and

Joseph felt on solid ground again. "It makes me humble," he exclaimed. "Ruby is the prettiest, the kindest, the funniest, the smartest girl I've ever known. Just being with her makes me... makes me want to stand up in worship service and lead a hymn of thanks."

"And you think she feels the same way about you?" Andy asked.

"I think she does." Joseph nodded. "*Ya*, I'm sure of it."

"And you can talk to her? Because I know... I know words don't always come easy to you."

"We talk all the time. I never get tired of talking to her. Sara has to come out and chase me off her porch when it's time for Ruby to go in. And if she'd let me, I'd be at her supper table every night just so I could look at Ruby."

Andy grimaced. "Sounds like you've got it bad. Like you were struck by a lightning bolt."

"It's what it feels like." Joseph was surprised by how easily he could voice his thoughts on Ruby. "I think about her first thing when I wake up in the morning, and I think about her all day. She's special, Andy. I know she's the one God wants me to choose for my wife." A black-and-white barn cat came over and rubbed up against Joseph's leg and he bent and stroked it. Joseph scratched it behind the ears and it began to purr loudly.

"So why doesn't Aunt Magdalena think she's a good match for you?" Andy asked. "I know she wants you to marry. She's always telling my mother how she wants you to settle down, find a good wife and give her grandchildren."

"I don't know why Mother doesn't approve of Ruby," Joseph admitted. "I think maybe she isn't happy because she didn't do the arranging."

"But it was *her* idea to go to the matchmaker, *ya*?"

"Right," Joseph agreed. "But I think she had it in her head that Sara was going to parade girls in front of her and she was going to pick for me."

Andy laughed. "Sounds like Aunt Magdalena."

"Anyway." Joseph gave a shrug. "Everything's going to work itself out. Mother invited Ruby to supper this evening." He looked down at his hay-flecked clothing and dirty shoes. "Which means I'd better get cleaned up. I know for certain that neither of them will allow me to sit at the table looking like this."

"And I'd better get on home," Andy said as they started across the barnyard.

"You know you're welcome to stay for supper."

Andy laughed. "Looking like this?"

"I can loan you some clean clothes," Joseph

offered. "And it would give you an opportunity to meet Ruby. See, I'm not trying to hide her."

"Not tonight, thank you. I promised my younger brothers and sisters I'd take them for pizza in Dover. Maybe another night we could go out together. You bring Ruby, I'll find a date, and we could go out to the mall and just walk around. Have a bite at the food court?"

"Maybe. I don't know how Ruby's parents feel about her going to malls and such."

Andy walked backward and shrugged. "I think Josie King might be having a singing next week. Maybe we could double-date for that?" The sound of a dinner bell rang out from the back porch.

"Joseph," Magdalena called. "Supper."

"Guess you best be going," Andy said.

Joseph thanked Andy again, then watched him stride off in the direction of his family's farm, before heading to the house. There, he found Ruby on the back porch waiting for him. Sara must have dropped her off while he was in the back field. "I'm glad you could come," he said. Just seeing her made him smile.

She grinned, clasping her hands together. "Glad you invited me."

They just stood there looking at each other until Joseph began to feel awkward. "Well, I—I better get washed up before we eat," he told her.

She was still smiling at him, which made him feel good. Capable. "You must be exhausted after throwing all that hay up into the barn."

He shrugged. "It's hard work, but it feels good when the barn is full and you know you have good hay for the horses and the cows for the winter." He gestured toward the door. "How is she? Is she in a good mood?"

It was Ruby's turn to shrug. "As good as mine."

He met her gaze questioningly.

"Don't worry." She gave a wave. "It's fine. There is bound to be a little—" She broke off at the sound of buggy wheels. "Expecting someone? Another girl maybe?" she teased.

"Never."

A buggy pulled by a gray horse was coming up the driveway. It was Elmer Raber. He waved with enthusiasm. "Not late for supper, am I?" he shouted as he rolled by.

"*Ne.* Just in time," Joseph replied. He glanced at Ruby and lowered his voice. "Did you know Elmer was coming?"

She shook her head. "Your mother didn't mention it."

Elmer drove his horse to the hitching post and climbed down from his buggy. "Joseph, come give me a hand. I've brought your mother a roast, a half-dozen steaks and some prime rib."

The back door opened and Magdalena came out. "Elmer!" she called, wiping her hands on her apron. "How pleasant to see you." She looked at Ruby. "Isn't this nice? Elmer's come to join us."

"Nice," Ruby repeated.

"You brought meat?" Magdalena called to Elmer. "Now, you know that wasn't necessary, but we do appreciate it."

"I can't bake a pie." Elmer wrapped the reins around the hitching post. "But I know a good roast when I see one."

Joseph's mother was all smiles, positively twittering as she said to Joseph, "Those two got along so well last time, Elmer and Ruthie—"

"Ruby," Joseph interrupted.

Magdalena gave a quick smile in Ruby's direction and went on talking. "I thought I'd invite him for supper. You never know. Men and women plan, but the Lord decides. Give Elmer a big, big welcome."

Joseph glanced at Ruby as he headed for the buggy to take the box Elmer was unloading from his buggy.

"You heard your mother, Joseph," Ruby said sweetly. "Let's give Elmer a big welcome."

"Ya," Magdalena waved her guest in. "Come right in and sit down, Elmer. You too, Ruby. Joseph can put the horse and buggy in the

shed. And while I get supper on the table, you two can have a nice talk."

"Thank you for the meal, Mother." Joseph rose from the kitchen chair he'd carried into the living room after the meal. "You outdid yourself as usual."

"Ya," Elmer agreed. "I don't know when I've eaten better." He stood up from the couch and scooped up the last few kernels of popcorn out of a bowl and put them in his mouth. "Good cooking, good talk and a good game. I can't think when I've enjoyed myself more."

Joseph picked up the last of the playing pieces and put them back into the box, relieved the evening was coming to an end. After they'd eaten, the four of them had played Settlers of Catan, a board game that Ruby and Elmer seemed to enjoy as much as he and his mother did. The thunderstorm that Joseph had worried over when he'd been getting up the hay had finally materialized. Now the thunder and lightning had moved off to the east, but a light rain continued to fall, which meant that he could couldn't drive Ruby home in the open wagon as he'd promised Sara. He wondered if he should ask his mother to ride with them in the buggy. It was the right thing to do; he just didn't know how Ruby would feel about it.

"Elmer, you know where the matchmaker lives, don't you? Would you mind dropping Ruby off at Sara's?"

"Um…sure," Elmer said, looking from Magdalena to Ruby and back to Magdalena again.

Ruby, who'd been carrying the empty popcorn bowl to the kitchen, let it slip through her fingers. The aluminum container hit the floor with a bang and bounced. Unpopped kernels rained on the floor. *"Ne,"* she managed as she grabbed the fallen bowl. The kernels rolled. "I wouldn't want to put you to the trouble."

"It wouldn't be any trouble," Elmer protested. "I just—"

"I… *I'm* taking Ruby home," Joseph interrupted. "Thank you… Elmer, but… Ruby is… She's my responsibility."

Ruby blushed and looked distressed. "I don't want to cause any problem," she said. "I can walk."

"Nonsense." His mother moved to Ruby's side and slipped an arm around her waist. "You'll not walk home in a rainstorm. There's no good reason you can't accept a ride from Elmer. The rules of courtship don't apply to friends. And Elmer is certainly in that category."

"I hope I'm a friend to all of you, Magdalena," Elmer said, looking to her.

"There." His mother released Ruby and put her hands together with a smile. "It's all settled."

"It is *not* settled," Joseph managed. "Ruby, Elmer, if you'll excuse us for just a moment, I need to speak to my mother. Alone."

"Certainly," Elmer replied.

Ruby looked as if she were about to burst into tears. Joseph met her gaze. "Just give me a moment," he said quietly to her. "I'll hitch up the buggy and take you. Sara will just have to understand."

"If you're sure," she said, glancing from him to his mother.

"I'm sure," Joseph said, and then he looked to Elmer. "Maybe you could take Ruby out on the back porch for me. I'll be right along."

Elmer nodded and motioned to Ruby. Together the two hurried into the kitchen and then out the back door.

"I never!" His mother crossed her arms over her chest. "How could you be so disrespectful to a guest in our house? And to me?"

Joseph bit back the hot retort that rose on his tongue. "Mother, for once will you just stop talking and let me speak my mind?"

"Joseph Brenneman. What would your father say if he heard you talking to me in such a tone?"

"He'd probably say that it was high time I stood up for myself."

"Where's the respect the Bible says you should show your mother?" She covered her face with her hands and began to weep softly.

The sound cut him sharply. He wanted to beg her forgiveness and tell her not to cry, that he'd do anything if she didn't cry. But he thought of Ruby standing on the back porch, he thought of her crying, and he stiffened his spine. "I do respect you, Mother."

"All I've ever done is love you and try to do what is best for you," she said into her hands.

"I know that. But you have to realize that I'm a man grown. Some things I have to decide for my own. And choosing a wife is one of those things." He wanted to put his arms around her and comfort her, but he didn't.

Another big sob. Her narrow shoulders trembled. "This isn't—isn't the way it was supposed to go."

"You are the one who urged me to go to Sara Yoder and find a wife." Joseph exhaled slowly and took a clean handkerchief from his pocket. He passed it to her and she blew her nose daintily. "Mother, you should be happy for me," he told her. "I've found the most wonderful girl, the sweetest—"

"Ugly," she whispered.

"What?" He drew back. "What did you say?" He couldn't believe what he'd just heard.

"She's—she's not even pretty. You'll have thick, unlovely children."

He blinked, still in disbelief. "Mother. How can you say that? Ruby's beautiful."

"You see?" She shook her head. "I believe you've lost your wits. She's as plain as an old shoe. Her mouth is too big, and her nose looks like a lump of biscuit dough. And her chin…" She gave another wail. "Stubborn. A stubborn chin."

"Don't ever speak about Ruby like that again. Do you hear me, Mother?"

She sniffed and blew her nose again. "Very uncharitable talk for a son to his widowed mother."

"We're not going to talk about charity, Mother. That you would say such things about the girl I love, the girl who is going to be the mother of your grandchildren, it—it hurts me more than I can tell you. I won't have it."

"And what about her cooking? Did you ever taste such terrible macaroni and cheese as what she brought tonight? Have you?"

He almost smiled. "I can't say I'm in love with her mac and cheese, but I am in love with her."

His mother wiped her eyes. "Not yet. Please

tell me that you aren't marrying her yet. You haven't even been to the bishop."

He sighed. "*Ne*, I haven't, but I will as soon as Ruby tells me that she's sure of me."

"You mean *she* hasn't agreed yet?" Suddenly she perked up. "So she's not sure?"

"We're courting, Mother. That means that we're trying to find out if we're right for each other, but both of us feel we're headed toward marriage. Now, I want you and Ruby to get to know each other, but if she isn't welcome here under your roof—" he took a breath "—then I'm not either."

"Not my roof," she said. She began to fan herself with her hand. "Yours, strictly speaking. I'm the dependent one, the widow with only one son to care for her. Helpless in my old age."

"Mother, you are far from helpless. You're strong and smart, and to me you've always been loving and charitable. I'm asking you to show some of that charity to the girl I want to marry."

"So you haven't set a date for the wedding?"

"*Ne*. Not yet, but—"

"Good, good. That's as it should be. Take your time. That's all I ask. Get to know her better. Find out something about her. Go and meet her family. See if she's all you think she is."

"That's the best advice you've given me all evening," he said. "Now, I'm driving Ruby home and then I'll be back. Don't wait up. I think you and I will both be in a better mood if we say good-night now and see each other fresh in the morning."

She brought a hand to her mouth. "I never meant to hurt your feelings, Joseph. You must know that. And it was never for myself. I could get used to plain grandchildren if—"

"Mother," he warned.

"Sorry. It just slipped out." She gathered her dignity around her and raised her chin higher. "That was ill said. I suppose we all have different ideas of beauty."

"Apparently." He headed for the door.

She followed him. "And beauty is fleeting. Not worth much compared to grace."

He didn't turn around. "Good night, Mother."

"Good night, Joseph."

Grabbing his hat, he stepped onto the porch and pulled the back door closed behind him. The rain was coming down harder, but Ruby and Elmer were standing far enough back that they were dry.

"Sorry about...that," Joseph murmured.

"It's fine." Ruby smiled up at him. "Elmer and I were just talking about the rain. He thinks it's going to be off and on for a while yet."

"Why don't I drive the both of you to the matchmaker's and then bring you back home,"

Elmer suggested. "My horse is already hitched up in the shed, and it would be the least I can do in exchange for that fine supper."

"Thank you," Ruby said, "but Joseph and I can manage in the wagon." She motioned to the rain slickers hanging on the porch wall. "The horse is going to be wet no matter what."

"Ne," Joseph said. "That's silly. I'll hitch up my buggy."

Ruby frowned. "I'm afraid Sara will be disappointed in us for breaking her rule. She wanted us to be chaperoned if we rode in a closed buggy."

"Then it's settled," Elmer chimed in jovially, bringing his hands together. "I've got no one waiting for me at home but my gray cat. I can be your chaperone and bring Joseph back." He chuckled as he adjusted his hat before stepping into the drizzle. "Who knows? I might even be invited back in for another slice of your mother's fantastic chocolate pie."

Chapter Eight

"Stay where you are," Joseph said, rising from his chair. "I'll get you a refill on your lemonade."

With a handful of napkins, Ruby mopped at the lemonade on the table and hoped that no one in the fast-food restaurant had noticed she'd spilled her drink. It was a Friday evening and she and Joseph, Leah and her beau and Joseph's cousin Andy and a young woman named Nancy had hired a van and driver to take them to Dover. They'd gone to an indoor produce market and then come to the restaurant for supper.

Joseph had just brought up the subject of visiting her parents. Again. And she wasn't sure what to say to him. For once her clumsiness had come in handy. When she'd knocked over the cup so hard that the lid popped off, both of them had jumped out of their chairs to keep from becoming covered in lemonade, ending the conversation. Or at least putting it off.

She watched Joseph walk away and when he turned to look at her, she couldn't help but smile back.

She supposed he was right. It probably *was* time he met her parents, but it made her nervous just thinking about it. So long as she was in Delaware, and her *mommi* and *daddi* were in Pennsylvania, she could almost forget that she wasn't being totally honest with Joseph about who she was. She *did* want them to meet Joseph. Of course she did. She wanted them to see how wonderful Joseph was and to agree that he would make the perfect husband for her. But when they met him, it would be time to tell him her secret and she wasn't looking forward to having to admit to him that, while perhaps she'd not been dishonest with him, she'd certainly not been as forthcoming with some information.

When they'd first met and she'd gotten to know Joseph at the hospital, she'd been instantly attracted to him. For her, it was love at first sight, the love that her mother talked about finding with her father. But with each day and week that she'd known Joseph, her feelings for him had become deeper, so much deeper that she'd realized her first infatuation had been a feeble emotion compared to how she felt now. Just the sight of him made her giddy. She thought about him all the time, and she dreamed about him at night.

They'd been eating their chicken sandwiches and fries, laughing and talking when Joseph had asked her if she'd contacted her parents about the two of them coming for a visit. She'd become so flustered that she'd spilled the large lemonade.

Ruby watched an English father walk by the table. He was carrying a small boy about two years of age, and he held the hand of a little girl a year or two older. The children were blond and blue-eyed and dressed alike in blue jeans and striped shirts. The girl's hair was pulled up into a ponytail and tied with a pink ribbon.

The little girl stared at her and pointed before breaking into a big smile. "Daddy, look. That lady has a bonnet like my Polly doll."

"She does," the father agreed, ushering her by.

Ruby smiled at the little girl. Ruby had worn her best go-to meeting clothes tonight, her good black bonnet and cape. No wonder the little English girl had thought she looked like a doll. Old Order Amish clothing did stand out in the outside world. But Ruby didn't mind. She liked being unique. It was part of who she was.

Didn't the Bible instruct them to remain apart from the world?

She glanced around to see what had happened to Joseph. He was standing in line behind a man in a military uniform and a woman with three half-grown children. Joseph smiled at her and she smiled back. How handsome he looked. A small wave of joy rippled under her skin and she hugged herself. How could a man like Joseph have chosen her? It had to be God's doing. Never had she ever expected, when she'd agreed to seek out a matchmaker, that she'd meet anyone like him, and not only *meet* him, but have him ask her to become his wife. Joseph was the answer to her prayers.

Ruby's *daddi* had always told her that the right man would come along and would love her despite her clumsiness and her plain face. Her *mommi* said that she was beautiful; it simply took a man with a pure heart to open his eyes and see. Until her teens, Ruby had never thought much about the way she looked. She knew she had her mother's square chin and her father's nose. But she was sturdy and bursting with energy and good health. As her mother said, she'd been fortunate enough to be born with two eyes that worked, two ears that heard the word of God, two good arms and two legs that carried her through the day. What did it matter if Mary Mast had flaxen hair and skin like new-skimmed cream? And many was the person with beautiful eyes who couldn't see a hand in front of their face. But when Ruby had blossomed from child to woman, being plain and sturdy rather than pretty suddenly mattered. It mattered when her friends all paired up and began to marry. It mattered when her mother's friends whispered behind their knitting and called her "poor Ruby" and said "too bad she didn't take after the other side of the family."

Ruby straightened and smiled, realizing that she wasn't "poor Ruby" anymore. Joseph loved her for who she was rather than what she looked like. Her parents had been right all along. When the right man came along, he didn't see a snub nose or a thick waist and wide feet. Knowing that Joseph thought she was beautiful made her feel beautiful and cherished. And if her mother and father had been right about this, maybe they were right about what they'd asked her to promise them.

The man and his children joined a fair-haired woman at a booth a short distance away. The little girl looked back and waved and Ruby waved back. She couldn't help thinking that maybe she and Joseph would be blessed with children. Maybe they would have a girl who looked like the English child, all blonde and blue-eyed and dimpled. Boy or girl, it wouldn't matter to her. They would welcome whomever God sent, and they would love the child, sick or well. If a baby were born to them who was little, like Ellie, or with Down syndrome like Susannah, Leah's sister, it wouldn't matter. Every baby, quick or slow, pretty or plain, was a bundle from heaven. All children came from God, and a special child would be cherished all the more. Still, she hoped Joseph's child might look like him, not because he was so attractive, but because she loved him so.

Joseph returned to the table with her drink refill and two ice-cream sundaes. "Sorry," he said. "There was a line at the counter."

"It's fine." She accepted the cup, setting it down on the table carefully. "I was watching that little English girl. She's adorable. She waved at me."

Joseph glanced at the booth she indicated. *"Ya,"* he agreed. "She is cute." And then he gave Ruby a smile that made her toes curl, but then he frowned. "Um. I…need to talk to you about something because… Well, I haven't been entirely honest with you, Ruby."

Her eyes widened. "You haven't? About what?" Her heart suddenly fluttered in her chest. "Oh, no, is this bad?"

"No, no, not bad. Not terrible. Just…" He

looked down at the table, slowly sliding her sundae to her. "It's just that earlier, when I brought up visiting your parents, I was hoping you'd say you were ready for me to meet them and we'd make plans. But actually…" He pressed his lips together. "I sort of already arranged for a driver to take us to Lancaster next week."

"You *sort of* arranged it?"

"I did. I made the arrangements, but we can… I can cancel." He grimaced. "I might have gotten a little ahead of myself. But, I *really* do want to meet your parents. And…and I think it's time." He met her gaze. "I'm sorry. For, you know, hiring the van before you and I… Well, before your parents agreed they wanted to meet me."

"Of course they want to meet you, Joseph. It's only that—" She was flustered. Not because she was nervous about her parents meeting him, but because that would make all of this real. And for it to be real, she'd have to tell him her history. All of it.

"Charley and Miriam, the couple that sponsored the schoolhouse painting frolic, said they could chaperone us on Saturday. I thought we could drive up together, and then Charley and Miriam will visit friends in the area. You and I can visit with your parents. We could take them out to eat, and we'll come back to Delaware in the evening."

"Oh," she said. "I'm sure they'd rather have dinner for us. I just I'll have tell Sara."

"You should tell your parents," he said. "If you think you're ready for me to meet them, of course. I just thought…I think we agreed that we both want to marry soon. Right?"

She looked down at the table. *"Ya."*

"So is that a yes? Can we go next Saturday?"

"Ya. I'm sure it will be fine. I just need to call and let them know. Leave a message on their answering machine. *Daddi* has a phone in the barn. For…emergencies and such. They can't wait to meet you," she added quickly.

"Good, then it's settled." Joseph laughed and scooped up a spoonful of vanilla ice cream with chocolate fudge sauce poured over it. He took a bite and said, "Don't look so worried. I'll be on my best behavior. But I'll warn you, we're not leaving until your father and mother give their blessing for us to marry." Then he slid his hand across the table and took her hand. "I'm not that bad of a prospect, am I?" he teased.

She shook her head. "They'll love you." She pulled her hand away and giggled self-consciously. Her hand still tingled from his touch. "Joseph, what will people say?" she whispered, glancing around the restaurant, but the other customers seemed to be concentrating on their own chicken and fries.

He chuckled. "I don't care. I'm not ashamed of letting them know how I feel about you."

As Ruby took a big bite of her own sundae, she couldn't help thinking that this Joseph Brenneman was so much more assured than the young man she'd nearly crushed when she'd fallen on him the first day they met. He hardly ever stammered when they were alone together, and he had no problems stating to her what he thought and how he felt. And being able to talk to each other was important in a marriage. She knew that from watching her parents.

"Hate to interrupt you two, but it's time to be heading back," came a raspy English voice behind her.

Startled, Ruby looked up to see their driver, Gene, standing beside the table. He was an older man with salt-and-pepper hair, a potbelly and a blue ball cap that read Niagara Falls. "The others are ready and my wife will be looking for me," he said heartily. "Early to bed, you know."

"Ya," Joseph agreed. "We'll be right behind you." He waited until the gentleman had walked away, then turned back to Ruby. "So it's settled, right? We visit your parents and as long as that goes well, we set a date for our wedding."

Ruby took a deep breath, almost feeling light-headed. Dreaming of a wedding was one thing, but the reality of it was quite another. Still, it was what she wanted more than anything. To marry Joseph. "It's settled," she agreed.

Ruby pressed her cheek against the cool glass window at the back of the van. It was raining, and the windows were steamed up and she was slightly carsick. She'd never particularly liked traveling by automobile, especially on gray days. She hoped it wasn't raining in Bee Bonnet, but she'd awakened to rain on Sara's roof, and so far the skies showed no signs of clearing.

It worried her that she hadn't had time to speak with her parents yet. She had hoped to talk to them and get their permission to tell Joseph what needed to be told so there would be no secrets on visiting day, but it had not been meant to be. On Monday, she'd walked to the chair shop and tried to reach them by phone. Like many folks in Bee Bonnet, they had a phone in the barn, which was used for business and emergencies. She had thought she might catch her father, but she hadn't and his answering machine hadn't been working. She'd then sent them a letter telling them she and Joseph were coming to visit, which was a good thing because on Wednesday she'd made a second attempt to call with the same results.

So Saturday had come, and here they were on their way to meet her parents in Pennsylvania. But it wasn't Miriam and Charley accompanying them; it was Magdalena.

"I wanted to surprise you," Magdalena had declared when Ruby had gotten into the van. "Won't this be fun? I can't wait to get to know your parents."

Helplessly, Ruby had looked at Joseph for an explanation, but he'd only rolled his eyes and given her a half-hearted smile.

"Already the first week of October," Madeline had proclaimed. "And harvest in full swing. You know Charley Byler has better things to do than tag along with you two to Lancaster County. They're a charitable couple, always thinking of others. But they have responsibilities. And Sara certainly can't object to Joseph's mother as a chaperone, can she?"

So the lovely trip, or what *should* have been a lovely trip, had been dominated so far by Magdalena, who'd gone so far as to plant herself beside her son in the middle bench seat, leaving Ruby to sit alone in the back. Magdalena hadn't stopped giving Joseph advice since they'd left Sara's.

"You need to be firm," she was saying. "Make it very clear that Ruby will be coming to live with you in Delaware. On no account will you be moving to Pennsylvania. You will be the husband, the head of the household. It's important that they respect you."

"*Ya*, Mother" Ruby heard Joseph reply.

"And ask questions about the family. What church community do they attend? How big is it? Are there any chronic illnesses in the family that we should be aware of?"

"*Ya*, Mother."

Joseph had barely said anything else in the first hour of the trip and Ruby wondered how he could be so agreeable. Yes, Magdalena was his mother, but he was a grown man. Ruby couldn't help but wonder if she was making a mistake in marrying Joseph. Was this what their marriage would be like? Would Magdalena always be at the center of their decisions? Would what his mother wanted come ahead of what she wanted?

"You know, Joseph," Magdalena continued, her voice growing louder and more insistent. "If you're not totally happy with what the Planks have to say, it's not too late to break this betrothal. Better safe than sorry, I always say."

"Coffee stop," Gene called from the driver's seat. He slowed the van and turned in to a convenience store. "Good doughnuts, clean restrooms. I always stop here when I'm passing through. Take your time. No hurry."

Joseph was waiting for Ruby when she

stepped down out of the van. "Would you like coffee or something cold to drink?" he asked. "Are you hungry? Would you like a doughnut?"

"A soda would be nice," Ruby answered. "But I don't want to eat anything. My mother will be certain to have dinner waiting for us. She'll be disappointed if we don't sit down with big appetites."

When they returned to the van, Joseph motioned her to the rear bench seat, but this time, he followed her and sat beside her. "What's wrong?" he asked. "You're being quiet. I thought you'd be excited to be seeing your parents today."

"I am," she said.

Magdalena stood on the step the driver had put out for them and looked into the van at the two of them. "Joseph? Aren't you sitting with me?" she called.

"*Ne*, I'm riding back here with Ruby."

"Suit yourself." Magdalena frowned and slid into the middle seat.

"Everyone buckled up?" Gene asked. He started the ignition. Soon they were back on the road and heading north.

Ruby and Joseph exchanged glances. Ruby slowly let out the breath she hadn't realized she'd been holding.

"So tell me what's wrong," Joseph said quietly.

"She wasn't supposed to come," Ruby whispered. "Miriam and Charley were supposed to be our chaperones." She wanted to say "This was supposed to be fun." But she didn't.

Joseph nodded. "I know, and I'm sorry. She didn't tell me that she was going to cancel on them and come herself."

"We should just have asked my parents to come to Delaware," Ruby said, glancing out the window. She knew there was no sense being upset with Joseph. He hadn't done this, but she didn't see why she couldn't be at least a little upset about the situation.

"What did you want me to do, Ruby? If I'd known, I would have stopped her. But I didn't. I didn't know until the van arrived and by then, she'd already canceled on Charley and Miriam. There was no way Sara was going to give her approval for us to travel by ourselves. What was I supposed to do?"

"Your mother doesn't like me," Ruby said, keeping her voice low. "She'll never like me."

He shook his head. "That's not true. How could she not learn to love you?"

"You agree with everything she says."

"*Ne*, Ruby, I don't. But I'm caught in the middle here. Think of how much you love your parents. I feel the same way about my mother." Their hands were side by side on the seat and he lifted one finger and stroked hers. "You'll have to learn to get along with her. You can speak up for yourself. I've seen you do it. And believe it or not, she admires a woman with spunk."

"I didn't plan for this," she replied. "I didn't tell my parents that your mother was coming."

"From what you've had to say about them, I'm sure they'll be fine with it," he said. "Now this is what it is. There's no reason to let her ruin our day. Let's make the best of it." He looked at her hopefully, sliding his hand over hers. "Please?"

Ruby stared at the front of the van where Magdalena was leaning forward and talking loudly into the driver's ear. Joseph was right. They would have to make the best of it, but she didn't feel much like being reasonable. She wanted to feel sorry for herself, to have Joseph take her side against his mother. But that wasn't the way she'd been raised. "I'm sorry for being out of sorts," she murmured, slipping her hand out from under his. If Magdalena saw them holding hands, there was no telling how she'd respond. "I'll try harder to be more understanding."

"Thank you," he said quietly. "I appreciate that. I know she isn't always charitable toward you, and that's wrong. But you have to put yourself in my place. I'm all she's got. It must be difficult for her. Everything will change when I marry you. She won't be the center of my world anymore. It will be you, Ruby. Because…because I love you."

Her eyes grew moist. It wasn't the Amish way to make such declarations.

She looked up into his handsome face. "Do you mean that? Because I love you too." Her last words came out in a whisper.

"I do mean it," he said. "I promise you that this will all work out. Because we do love each other. I just ask that you don't ask me to hurt her or make her feel unneeded. Once she comes to realize what you mean to me, she'll treat you the way you deserve to be treated. You haven't always seen the best side of my mother, but she's a wonderful person. And she has a loving heart."

"Like I said, I'll try to be more understanding," Ruby promised, her heart still fluttering from hearing him say he loved her. "And I'll pray harder," she added.

"Ya," he agreed. "And so will I. I love you both, and I want you to become close."

"What are you two whispering about back there?" Magdalena called.

"Prayer, Mother," Joseph answered.

"Goot," Magdalena answered. "We should all pray for guidance. We need to know if this marriage is God's will or if you two aren't just infatuated with each other."

Ruby and Joseph looked at each other.

"It isn't," he mouthed and she smiled.

"I'll try harder," she repeated.

And the way he looked at her made her realize she'd do anything he asked, just so she could be with him forever and always.

The landscape out the windows of the van had become hilly with fields of corn shocks, stone farmhouses, red barns and the occasional gray buggy pulled by a high-stepping horse. Sometime after they'd crossed the state line into Pennsylvania, the sun had come out from behind the clouds and the day had turned from gloomy to glorious and sunny.

Ruby sat up straighter and stared out at the familiar sights. Soon there were signs for Bird in Hand and Lancaster and Strasburg. "You go toward Strasburg," she called to the driver. "Then when you reach the crossroads just east of town, you make a left turn on Green Willow Road."

"I've got the address in my GPS. They live on Bee Bonnet Road, right?"

"Once you reach Bee Bonnet Road, it's about four miles," Ruby explained. "The place is on the right, back a long lane, but there's an old mill just off the road. You can't miss it. There are two houses. One is stone and the other smaller one is frame."

What would her parents think of Joseph? Surely Magdalena would like them. Who wouldn't like her *mommi* and *daddi*? Everyone in Bee Bonnet said how pleasant they were.

At last Gene drove around a bend and down a hill beside a rocky creek. Ahead was the old stone mill and just before the mill, the driveway that led to the farm where she'd grown up. Ruby was so excited she could hardly stand it. Without realizing what she was doing, she reached over and gave Joseph's hand a squeeze.

Gene turned into the long driveway.

"Quite some farm," Magdalena remarked.

And it was, Ruby thought. White fence posts enclosed herds of dairy cows, horses and beef cattle. Sheep grazed on the slope that ran down to the creek. Straight rows of corn shocks stretched as far as the eye could see. And nestled against a rise of ground stood a big stone house that had been there for nearly two hundred years. It was flanked by a slowly turning windmill, two massive barns, a half-dozen outbuildings and a smaller house.

"Your parents live here?" Joseph asked as he took in the bounty of rich land and fertile fields.

Before she could think how to answer, the side door opened on the smaller house and out came her parents, her father pushing her mother's wheelchair. Both of them were waving, smiles from ear to ear.

Ruby wiggled past Joseph and jumped out almost before the van had stopped rolling. *"Mommi!"* she cried. *"Daddi!"* She ran to them and threw her arms around first one and then the other.

"Where's this young man of yours?" her father demanded, grinning.

"So you got my letter. I called, but—"

"Of course we got your letter. Been looking forward to this all week. So where is he?" her father asked. "You didn't lose him on the way, did you?"

Ruby was laughing and weeping with joy at the same time. *"Ne,* I didn't. This is my—" She broke off as she saw that it wasn't Joseph climbing down from the van but a stern-faced Magdalena. "This is Magdalena," she corrected herself. "Joseph's mother."

"Welcome to our home," her father said. "What a pleasant surprise."

Joseph stepped out behind Magdalena and gave an uncertain smile.

Ruby could see that he was nervous, and she prayed silently that his words wouldn't lodge in his throat nor that his shyness would make this meeting uncomfortable. "And *this* is my—" she began again.

"My son, Joseph," Magdalena finished for her. "He's a little backward when it comes to strangers, but I assure you, the boy has all his wits."

"Joseph! A good name for a young man," Ruby's father exclaimed. "An excellent name. You see, *Mommi*, he's all our Ruby said he was." He extended a hand to Joseph and the two shook hands vigorously.

"*Mommi*, you look wonderful." Ruby hugged her mother a second time. "How I've missed you and *Daddi*. I've so much to tell you."

"Gracious, child, don't they feed you in Delaware? Look at her, Solomon. I believe she's lost twenty pounds since she's been away," her mother proclaimed.

Ruby laughed. "I wish. And you know I haven't." She kissed her mother's cheek. "Magdalena, this is my mother, Ina." She turned to smile at Joseph's mother. "I hope you two will become friends," she said.

Magdalena's eyes narrowed thoughtfully. "Well, certainly, certainly we'll have a lot to talk about. I've much to ask you, Ina."

"Ask away," her mother replied. "Questions are free, but I warn you, answers cost a dollar."

Magdalena looked puzzled, but Ruby's father laughed. "That's my Ina," he said. "Always teasing. Now, you behave yourself, wife. What will our guests think of us? And worse, what will they think of our daughter?"

What indeed, Ruby wondered as her mother clapped her hands and ushered them all around the house to the picnic table where a huge lunch was waiting. She'd hoped to speak to her parents in private before the visiting began. She really felt it was time to tell Joseph the truth about her situation and her past, but she wanted their permission. Obviously there would be no time for that now. She'd just have to hope for the best. *Ne*, she thought, not hope but pray. She'd pray everyone had a good afternoon and that everything would work itself out, including her secret. Because if her marriage to Joseph was meant to be, it was meant to be.

God's will, she told herself. *God's will.*

Chapter Nine

Joseph took a seat at the picnic table under the poplar tree and tried not to show how nervous he was. Ruby's parents seemed welcoming and pleasant, but he was still sweating beneath his hat's brim. He wanted to make a good impression, and as his mother had reminded him in front of everyone, he wasn't at his best with strangers. But he was determined that this would be different. His and Ruby's future was at stake. She was depending on him, and he couldn't let her down. One way or another, he would fight through his shyness and be the man she deserved. He'd ask her father for her hand in marriage. God willing, he thought and offered a silent prayer.

Joseph suddenly realized that Ruby's father was speaking to him, and gave the older man his full attention.

"...heard so much about you," Solomon went on heartily. "*Hallich* we finally get to meet you."

Joseph nodded and opened his mouth to make some kind of proper response, but when nothing came out, Solomon went right on talking without missing a beat. The older man didn't seem to notice that he was the only one speaking, which was fine with Joseph.

Ruby's father was a solid man in his late sixties with a full beard and bushy gray eyebrows that arched up at the outer corners. He had full red cheeks, a wide mouth and a nose much like Ruby's. Solomon was clearly a man who liked his food and liked to laugh, and he obviously was as fond of his daughter as his wife seemed to be because both of them kept smiling at Ruby with genuine pleasure.

"It's good of you...to have us visit," Joseph managed when Solomon stopped talking long enough to catch a breath.

Solomon grinned, slapped Joseph on the back and shoved a huge mug of cider into his hand. "Taste that. Cider. Sweet. Not hard. I don't hold with spirits. What do you think? Secret recipe. You have to marry into the *familye* to get it." He chuckled, a deep, rumbling belly laugh that threatened to pop the buttons of his old-fashioned, long-sleeved blue shirt. "And even then, maybe not until we have a few grandbabies."

"Solomon, no need to talk of *kinner* yet," Ruby's mother said. "You'll frighten the young man away."

"I don't think so," Solomon replied. "He's smitten. Look at him, *Mommi*. He can't take his eyes off our Ruby."

Ina laughed, a loud, jolly sound. Joseph hadn't expected the wheelchair. Ruby hadn't mentioned that her mother had health problems. But Ina didn't look sick or feeble. Her cheeks were full of color, her skin clear and her hair, although streaked with gray, was thick and shining, framing a square, pleasant face. He wondered why Ina couldn't walk but didn't want to ask such a personal question.

"*Buwe* or *maed*, we don't care," Solomon continued merrily. "Boy or girl. We're not getting any younger and we'd like to bounce some *kinner* on our *gnie* while we've still got the energy. Not that we expect you to have more than five or six. Families aren't as large as they once were, not even in Bee Bonnet. Why, when I was a tad, it was nothing to see a family of fourteen kids. But things are different now. Six would be *goot*. Excellent. Maybe three boys and three girls. What do you think?"

"*Daddi*, please," Ruby pleaded jokingly. "Don't run Joseph off before he's even had his dinner." She didn't seem in the least embarrassed by her father's remarks.

"She's right, Solomon." Ina waved a finger at her husband. "Give Ruby's young man a chance to eat his dinner before you start naming their firstborn. And speak English or *Deitsch* but not both at the same time. Our visitors will think this is an uncivilized household Ruby comes from."

"Whatever you say, *Mommi*." Ruby's father's reply was so meek that even Joseph couldn't keep a smile off his face, because even he could see that Solomon wasn't in the least repentant, and Ina wasn't in the least offended.

A cement sidewalk and patio made it easy for Ruby's mother to whip around the picnic table, directing everyone to seats and rolling up to take her place at the end of the table opposite her husband. There seemed to be nothing frail about Ina. Rather she appeared quite hearty with her ample girth and cheery countenance. Had she been standing upright instead of sitting in the wheelchair, he guessed she was taller than her husband. And she had the arms of a blacksmith.

Joseph glanced at his mother, who'd ignored the chair Ina had pointed to and taken a place smack-dab between him and Ruby. His mother was smiling her practiced smile and taking in the yard and the small house and neat garden with a calculating eye. He knew she was comparing the Plank's home to the larger stone house that stood not far away. *Be nice*, he wanted to say to her, but of course, he couldn't.

But his mother had turned her attention to Ina. She'd always had compassion for the sick or handicapped. And she was always the first to respond to a neighbor or friend's health crisis. Nothing was too much to do for someone in trouble. His mother had so many admirable qualities. Why couldn't she show them to the woman he loved?

"You have a fine garden," his mother remarked to Ina. "How do you manage?"

"*Ach*, goodness. *Ne*, that isn't my garden," Ina answered. "I wish it was. I've been after Solomon to build me one of those raised vegetable beds so that I can keep my hand in. The garden belongs to my twin sister, Ellen. She lives here with us, though she's gone today. She has a fair hand with anything that grows. Just don't put her in a kitchen. She cooks like a bishop's wife."

"The bishop's wife—that's a family joke," Solomon explained with a chuckle. "You see, the last two bishops we've had, their wives were good-hearted for certain, but they couldn't boil water." His ample belly quivered with suppressed laughter. "So, I always say Ellen—"

"If you can't say anything *goot*," Ina interrupted.

"Is a kindhearted woman," Solomon finished with a nod. "That's what I was going to say." He exchanged glances with Ruby and both chuckled. "You're too quick to judge me," he told his wife. "And me as innocent as a deacon on the Sabbath."

"Your words maybe, but not your thoughts." Ina shook her head. "You will have to excuse my husband," she went on good-naturedly. "Sometimes, he acts as though he's never grown up."

"I like to have a little fun." He winked at Joseph. "And what's wrong with that? Especially on this special day with Ruby's Joseph and his mother?"

Joseph looked at his mother, who seemed to him anything but at ease among these lighthearted people. She was sitting primly, hands folded in her lap, mouth turned up in a polite smile. She always admonished him about being easier with strangers, but he knew her well enough to see that she was nervous too.

"So let's get down to business. When will you be taking this girl off my hands?" Solomon asked Joseph the moment they'd finished the silent grace.

"Daddi!" Ruby blushed, this time definitely embarrassed. "Please. Not during dinner."

"Solomon," Ina admonished. "I told you. No talk of that at the table."

"Oh, all right," he responded, passing the potato salad to Joseph. "But we'll talk about it after, won't we, young man?"

Solomon laughed again, but from the look on Magdalena's face, Joseph was afraid that she hadn't understood he was joking with them.

Ina pushed a large platter of roast beef into his mother's hands. *"Picalilli,"* she said, dismissing the subject. "The young ones haven't said they are absolutely settled on the match yet. Have they, Solomon? They're only courting."

Solomon looked at Ruby. "Now, Ina, have you looked at our girl? Has she taken her eyes off him? Remember how you were when I went to your father to ask his blessing? Head over heels for me." He patted his stomach. "You wouldn't believe it, but I cut quite the figure when I was *rumspringa*. But that's all in the past now." He buttered a sweet-potato biscuit. "Some thought I was the catch of Lancaster County."

Ina laughed and shook her head. "Shame on you for saying such things."

He sighed. "No harm in telling the truth. But as I was about to say, our Ruby's just like her mother. A long time to decide on a man, but when she does, she won't be moved." His tone grew serious. "And a *goot* thing, I should say. Ina and me, we've knocked along pretty good, haven't we, wife? Through sickness and health, loss and God's bounty. A good match is a good match." He met his wife's gaze, his tone softening. "I knew it the day you said you'd marry me, *Mommi*."

"I…I can see you've had your share of troubles," Joseph's mother said, clearly uncomfortable with this tender exchange between husband and wife. "But all the more reason these two shouldn't rush into any commitment. It's plain that you need your daughter's help around here. I don't know how you've gotten along these weeks without her. And it's a child's duty to care for a parent. There's no question of my Joseph leaving his home and business. I'd not want her to marry him, move off to Delaware and leave you—"

"Ham, Magdalena?" Ina's eyes twinkled with mischief as she interrupted, plopping a wedge onto his mother's plate. "And do have some of those baked beans. They're Solomon's specialty. He made a fresh batch this morning."

"Your husband cooks?" his mother asked, drawing herself up in surprise.

Little beads of perspiration began to pop up above her upper lip and Joseph feared it would only be a matter of time until she began fanning herself with whatever she could find available.

"Some things better than me," Ina admitted.

"You're better than you were when we first married," Solomon teased. "And I don't cook too much, but what I do, I do *goot*. Best baked beans you ever wrapped your teeth around. I wanted to be certain there was plenty to eat."

Joseph surveyed the table. There were only five of them, but there was enough food to feed half the neighborhood. It smelled delicious, but he was too nervous to have much of an appetite. He sipped at the sweet cider, wishing that he and Ruby were anywhere else. Alone. He never felt ill at ease when it was just the two of them. Unconsciously he tapped one heel nervously against the cement deck. It was cool here in the shade of the trees, but waves of heat still radiated under his skin. He wondered if Ruby's parents could see him sweating. He hoped they didn't think him a complete clod.

"Raisin bread!" Solomon practically threw the bread trencher to Joseph. "Have some. And don't short yourself on Ina's cream cheese. She makes it herself from her grandmother's recipe."

"I have a good recipe for cream cheese too," Magdalena said. "I like to add herbs to mine, chives or sometimes rosemary."

"That sounds lovely," Ina said. "And do you make chowchow in Delaware?"

"*Ya*, we do. But Ruby brags on yours," his mother replied. The two women chatted about recipes and the benefits of an extensive herb garden for both cooking and medicinal needs for a few minutes. They were almost through the meal when Magdalena excused herself from the table. Joseph couldn't hear what she whispered to Ina, but the older woman pointed to the house.

"Just through the kitchen," Ina said. "You can't miss it. It's the only room with a bathtub."

"So tell the truth, you are talking about marriage, you and my daughter, aren't you?" Joseph heard in his ear as he watched his mother disappear into the little house.

"What?" Blinking, Joseph turned to Solomon. "I'm sorry. What were you saying?"

"Solomon," Ina warned. "Enough with that talk."

Her husband laughed like a boy caught with his hand in the sugar bowl, and she and Ruby chuckled with him. No one at the table but Joseph seemed surprised that Ina would repeatedly admonish her husband in public or that he would take it without offense. "My fault," Solomon said, holding up both hand, palms out.

"Finish up, young man. We've lots to discuss over *apfelstrudel* and *krum kuchen*."

"You can have one or the other, but not both," Ina cautioned. "You know what the doctor told you about your weight." She smiled at Joseph. "Of course, you can have as many desserts as you can hold. A trim young man like you. No need for you to worry about putting on pounds."

A sound came from inside the house like a piece of furniture being moved or maybe a door being opened. Joseph glanced nervously in that direction, then at Ruby.

She didn't seem to have heard the sound. "Joseph works hard," she put in. "He's busy all the time."

Joseph gathered his courage and looked up at her father. "I have a—a trade," he managed.

"You like to trade, do you?" Solomon asked, straight-faced. "Horses or cows?"

"Ne," Joseph replied. "I mean—"

"Daddi! Please. You know what Joseph was trying to tell you. He's a master mason. He's saying he can provide for a wife. Financially."

Joseph nodded gratefully. Where had this beautiful girl been all his life? Then another sound came from the house. Definitely a cupboard door being closed. Where was his mother? Why hadn't she come back outside?

"Glad to hear it," Solomon said, seeming to

take no notice of the sounds coming from the house, sounds that should not have been heard if someone was just using the bathroom.

"A man who won't work isn't worth his salt," Solomon went on. "He's certainly not worth my Ruby." He threw his daughter an adoring look. "One chick is all we have. Came later in life than we expected. God was good enough to spare us this one, and we cherish her. Not just any husband will do for our girl. I'm just saying…if you're considering marrying our Ruby."

"*Daddi*, I brought Joseph here so you could meet him. So you could get—" Ruby broke off as the sound of breaking glass came from inside the house. She and her mother both looked toward the house.

Joseph closed his eyes, not sure what to do. What to say. There was no way Solomon and Ina hadn't heard that. And they had to have realized that Magdalena was snooping. He cringed inwardly. How could she?

There was another clunk and the creak of a door. For an instant, Joseph thought he caught a glimpse of a face peering through an upstairs window. Hadn't Ina directed his mother to a bathroom downstairs? He hoped he was wrong and that someone else was inside.

"Ruby," Ina said. "I think Magdalena must be

lost. Excuse us," she said. "We'll go and show her the way out."

Ruby nodded and rose. She took hold of her mother's wheelchair and pushed her back along the sidewalk.

"I'm sorry," Joseph blurted. "My mother, she…" He didn't know what to say.

"Nothing to be sorry for," Solomon answered kindly. A large, red-combed rooster strolled up to the table, stopped by Ruby's father's chair and ruffled his feathers. "All right, all right," Solomon said, throwing the bird a handful of bread.

Joseph glanced at the house again. With the women gone, this was his opportunity to speak alone with Ruby's father. It might be his only opportunity today and, as he told Ruby, he wasn't leaving without bringing up his intentions. Formally. But his palms were sweaty and… "I want—want you to know, Solomon, how…wonderful Ru-Ruby is. I—I think she's wonderful."

Solomon beamed. "She is, isn't she?" He arched a bushy eyebrow. "Of course, she's can't cook very well—takes after her aunt Ellen. And she's not much of a seamstress either. Takes after her mother on that one, I'm afraid. For years I walked around looking like I'd sewn my own trousers with a pitchfork."

"I—I don't care," Joseph managed, feeling

sweat bead on his forehead under the brim of his hat again. "I—I think she's—she's perfect."

"And so you should." Solomon chuckled. "At least in the beginning years."

"I..." Joseph's mouth went dry and he could feel sweat trickling down the back of his neck. "I... While we're alone, I wanted to..." He took a deep breath and went on faster than before. "I—I'm asking for—for your permission...to marry Ruby."

Solomon's hazel eyes grew serious. "Your mother doesn't seem too pleased with your marrying. Or maybe it's Ruby she doesn't like. Does that matter to you?"

"*Ne*, it doesn't. But—but I don't think she dislikes Ruby." Joseph concentrated on what he wanted to say, trying not to stammer. "They just have to get to know each other, and—and learn to appreciate how special they both are. I know..." He glanced toward the house. "Maybe you haven't seen the best side of my mother. But I can tell you that she's a fine woman, and the most—most selfless mother any child could have. It's been just the two of us, the two of us since my father's death, and she—she's sacrificed a lot for me."

Ruby's father seemed to consider that. He took a slice of raisin bread and spread it with cream cheese. He took a bite, chewed and then nodded. "You and my daughter are of age. You don't need my permission to marry. And you certainly don't need your mother's." He took a bite of the bread. "Ruby has a good head on her shoulders. And you seem a sensible lad, as well. I trust Ruby's decision." He looked up at Joseph and broke into a kind smile. "But, for what it's worth, son, you have my blessing."

Ruby pushed the wheelchair to the door but stopped short of the entranceway. "Do you like him?" she asked her mother quietly. "Can you see how wonderful he is?"

From inside the house came the sounds of rustling and a scraping drawer.

"Are you sure this is what you want?" Her mother placed a soft hand over hers. "Dealing with that one in there may not be easy," she replied, indicating the house. "You can tell she's used to having things her way. And clearly she's nosy. You said she'll be living with you."

"We'll be fine, *Mommi*." Ruby nodded. "I'll win her over, you'll see. Magdalena's not a bad person. She's just strong-willed. But so am I. We'll find a way to make it work. We have to because we both love Joseph."

Ina eyed the door, then looked back at her daughter. "Best do it before you wed."

"But you see why I picked him, don't you?"

Ruby rested her hand on the back of her mother's wheelchair. She wanted to talk about Joseph, not about Magdalena. "Don't you think he's perfect?"

Her mother smiled up at her. "I can see you're in love."

Suddenly, Ruby was worried. Her smile fell. "You don't object to him, do you?"

"Of course not. If you're happy, Ruby, so are we. I think you've done exactly what we hoped you would do, find someone who would love you for yourself."

She let out a sigh of relief. "*Ya*, isn't it great? And he's going to ask *Daddi* for his permission to marry me."

"If your father will let him get a word in sideways."

She leaned close to her mother's ear and whispered. "So, now is it all right if—"

"Ruby!" The door opened, and then closed. "I…I…" Magdalena peeked through the screen. "I got quite turned around."

"But did you find what you were looking for?" her mother asked sweetly. "Upstairs?"

"What?" Magdalena pushed open the door again and stood staring at them. "I couldn't… That is, I was thirsty. I'm afraid I brushed against a canning jar…on the kitchen counter. It broke. I had to search for a…"

"A broom?" her mother suggested.

"Ya," Joseph's mother agreed. "A…a broom. And a dustpan."

"But you found the bathroom?" Ruby asked. She wondered how much of her conversation with her mother Magdalena had overheard. None of it, she hoped. But Magdalena had managed to appear at exactly the wrong time.

"No need for the two of you to leave your lunch. I was coming right back," Magdalena said.

"Of course, of course," her mother soothed. "We don't want to leave the men folk alone too long. They'll be talking business at the table again. You know how they are." She waved her hand and the three of them headed for the backyard.

When they reached the table, Ruby looked at Joseph, trying to see if she could tell if he'd had the nerve to ask her father for permission to marry and if he'd been successful. But her *Daddi* was telling a funny story about a deacon and an *Englisher* who'd gotten his car stuck in the cow pasture, and Joseph was giving him his complete attention.

Ruby's mother tried to engage Magdalena in small talk about the advantages of making coleslaw with lemon juice rather than vinegar, but Joseph's mother seemed determined to remain aloof. Maybe because she'd gotten caught snooping in the house. Ina, however, refused to take offense and launched into a long recitation of the bishop's last sermon and how well it was received by a visiting family from Ohio. Before Ruby knew it, they'd finished dessert and everyone chipped in to clear the table and carry the dirty dishes and the remainder of the food into the kitchen.

Ruby tried to get her mother alone again to ask about telling Joseph their secret, but Magdalena remained stuck to her side like glue. Time seemed to fly and the next thing Ruby knew, she heard a horn beeping and saw the van was rolling up the driveway.

"Here's your ride," Ruby's mother announced. "It seems like you just got here. Next time you and Joseph must come and stay with us for the whole weekend."

"They have to have a chaperone," Magdalena reminded her. "It isn't decent, otherwise. We keep by the old ways. People will talk, and it will do your daughter no good to get a name for being fast. Delaware isn't Lancaster, you know."

"So true. It isn't," her mother replied with a smile. "And thank the good Lord for it."

Feeling emotional at the idea of leaving, it was all Ruby could do to hold back her tears as she said her goodbyes and got into the van. Seeing her parents had been wonderful, but leaving them was difficult. She worried about their welfare, and she hadn't even gotten to see Aunt Ellen, who'd always been a big part of her home life.

She leaned close to the back window and waved at her parents. Her father was standing behind her mother's wheelchair, one hand on her shoulder. Her mother was doing her best to remain cheerful, but her smile was a mixed one. She knew they were happy for her and that they approved of Joseph, but she also was aware of how much her absence affected their daily life.

Joseph followed his mother into the van, gave a final wave and slid the door closed behind them.

"Why don't you sit here, Mother?" Joseph waved to the seat in the middle of the van, behind the driver. "It's not so bumpy here and you can see out the windows." He glanced over his mother's head and met Ruby's gaze, silently conveying that he was coming back to be with her.

But Magdalena had other ideas. "*Ne*, I'd rather sit with the two of you," she informed him. "It's nicer than sitting all alone. That way we can all chat." And with that, she moved to the back and plopped down on the bench seat beside Ruby.

"Would you like to sit by the window?" Ruby offered.

Magdalena shook her head and smiled. "*Ne*, I'll just sit between you. That way I won't have a bit of trouble hearing what's said."

Disappointment flickered briefly across Joseph's features, but then he smiled at his mother. With a slight shrug and an embarrassed smile, he slid his tall frame into the seat.

Ruby pressed her forehead to the window and stared out as the van rolled down the drive and away from her home and parents. She would have to write to them. She'd tell them how happy Joseph made her and how he was the answer to her dreams. Surely, that would be enough for her parents to release her from her promise. It had to be, because she couldn't go on like this. She couldn't keep deceiving Joseph. He was too fine a man to deserve such treatment, and she couldn't continue with the courtship without being completely honest with him.

That decision made, she felt a little better. She even managed a smile when Joseph caught her attention. Of course she would have managed an even bigger smile for him if he hadn't left her to sit beside his mother.

Chapter Ten

~~

"There." Sara tightened the last lid on the second batch of perfectly halved pears and added them to the ten quarts already cooling on the kitchen counter. "Don't they look nice?"

"Ya," Ruby agreed. Sara's canned pears were as pretty as a picture, all topped with colorful, strawberry-patterned lids. It was the week after her nerve-racking trip home to Bee Bonnet with Joseph, and she was helping Sara and the girls can.

Of all a woman's traditional chores, canning was Ruby's favorite. And canning with Sara and her new friends Leah and Ellie added to the enjoyment. Ruby didn't mind that canning was heavy, labor-intensive work because, unlike scrubbing floors, which had to be done over and over if you wanted to keep a decent kitchen, you could enjoy the results of a day's canning for months to follow. There was something so satisfying about knowing that the pantry shelves were stocked with good, nourishing food to share with friends and family.

Plus, she loved canned pears, especially in the dead of winter. There was something about the taste of pears that satisfied her sweet tooth without making her feel guilty for having a second helping of dessert. And best of all, when she was canning, she rarely dropped or broke anything. Today had been no exception—as long as she didn't count her stumble coming in from the porch when she'd sent a peck of Seckel pears rolling all over the kitchen floor.

But Sara, Leah and Ellie had only laughed and Ellie said it was a good thing no one sent her to gather the eggs. Everyone had taken her clumsiness so calmly that she'd found herself laughing with them as she crawled under a table to retrieve the last of the runaway pears.

Ellie was home this afternoon to help because she'd declared half days for the school all week. Ruby had come to be very fond of the woman from Wisconsin. Wherever Ellie was, there was always laughter, singing and fun. Normally, Ellie would be busy teaching at midday on a Wednesday, but so many of her older students were needed at home for harvest, canning and child care that Ellie thought it seemed wiser to start class an hour early and let all the children out at noon. A stern reminder to parents on the importance of regular attendance on the half days had so far proved successful. No one was falling behind in lessons and the families had the extra hands they needed so badly at this busy time of year.

"Ruby, stir that pear butter, will you?" Sara asked. "And taste it. I put in a little orange zest. See if it needs more." As usual, Sara was a bundle of energy, buzzing around the kitchen, directing the operation, cutting vegetables for a lamb stew for supper and planning the menu and activities for Saturday's upcoming haying day.

Leah and Ellie began singing a fast hymn as they worked together to fill the clean jars with fruit and pear juice. Some cooks used a thin sugar water to cover the fruit for canning, but not Sara. She preferred using not-so-perfect pears to make juice. She had told Ruby, "The good Lord has blessed me with a full head of good teeth. I mean to try to keep them. Too much sugar ruins a sweet smile."

Ruby joined in the praise hymn with Ellie and Leah as she stirred the bubbling pear butter. She knew the words by heart, and even though the kitchen was steamy and warm despite the crisp fall day, she was having a wonderful time. The smells coming from the kettle were amazing. In fact, the whole house smelled delicious.

There was only one thing keeping her day from being perfect and that was her worry concerning Joseph. Since they'd returned from visiting her parents, he'd been pressing for her to set a wedding date. Becoming his wife would be a dream come true, but there was still the concern that she hadn't been entirely forthcoming with him. She'd tried to call her parents the previous day and then she'd sent a letter asking them to release her from her promise. To add to her worries, somewhere in the back of her head, she kept thinking about Magdalena and Joseph's relationship with her. He told her that she would come first and his mother second after they were wed, but she wondered if she was being naive to think that was true.

"Look who's coming up the lane," Sara observed loudly. "Unless my eyes are getting as rusty as my knees, that's Joseph Brenneman's horse and buggy."

"Somebody's beau's come calling in the middle of a workday," Leah teased.

Ruby dropped the long-handled wooden spoon and ran to the window. Joseph's buggy was almost in the barnyard. She dashed to the bathroom. "Tell him I'm coming!" she sang, excited and giddy. She splashed water on her face, retied her headscarf and gave a quick glance into the small round mirror over the sink. She didn't have time to change her oldest dress for something nicer, but she could take off the pear-stained apron.

"You don't have to rush," Ellie said as Ruby hurried back through the kitchen. "That one's not going anywhere until he sees you."

"What are you doing here in the middle of the workday?" Ruby asked as the porch door banged shut behind her. She took the two bottom steps in one leap and met him halfway to the buggy.

"I needed to order extra bricks and was passing by Sara's so I thought…" Joseph was grinning shyly. Glancing toward the house, he motioned to her. "Come around to the other side of the buggy."

Curious, Ruby followed him. "Why? What is it?"

Joseph leaned in and picked up something. When he turned back to her, he was holding a bunch of black-eyed Susans. "I saw these in a field," he said, his voice husky. "It's late for them to still be blooming, but it was a sheltered hollow. I thought they were pretty. And—" he swallowed and handed her the flowers "—they reminded me of you. Because—because you're so beautiful."

Emotion made her throat tickle and brought tears to her eyes. No one but Joseph and her parents had ever called her beautiful. She knew it wasn't true. She was ordinary, not gorgeous like Leah or cute like Ellie. But it was so sweet to have Joseph say she was beautiful, and it made her feel all warm and fuzzy inside. "Thank you…for the flowers. They're wonderful." It wasn't enough. She wanted to say that she loved him more than hot raisin bread, but before she could get up the nerve to say it, he was swinging up into the buggy.

"Got to run," he said. "The guys are waiting for me. But I'll see you soon. And we'll set that date, won't we?" He threw her an adoring look, clicked to the horse and flicked the leathers over the standard bred's back. She stood there clutching her flowers and feeling so happy that she could almost float off the ground as the buggy rolled away.

Ellie's voice came from the porch. "Ooh, somebody got flowers. Pretty fancy."

"Ya," Ruby answered. She glanced down at the black-eyed Susans in her arms.

"You'd better get those in water," Ellie advised.

"What did he want?" Leah asked when Ruby returned to the kitchen.

She looked helplessly at Sara. "He wants to set a wedding date."

Ellie found an empty canning jar and filled it with water. "Here, put those in here. They wilt fast if they dry out."

"And there's something wrong with setting a date?" Sara asked. "Not having second thoughts, are you? Because if you have the slightest doubt, now's the time to speak up. I already told you I think this is fast for a couple who've only known each other as long as you two have."

Ruby shook her head. "Not having second thoughts about Joseph. I couldn't ask for a finer man."

"Very romantic for an Amish boy." Ellie took the flowers from Ruby to arrange in the jar. "Who would have thought he had it in him?"

"It's the shy ones who can fool you," Leah said.

"Ah, what's that smell?" Sara exclaimed. "Don't tell me the pear butter is burning." She darted to the stove, grabbed the spoon and stirred the mixture. "Just in time," she pronounced as she turned off the burner under the pot.

"*Ach*, it's getting warm in here," Ellie said. "Anyone for a cold glass of cider?"

"And some ginger cookies?" Leah suggested, grabbing a container from the cupboard.

"Absolutely," Sara agreed, going into the refrigerator for the glass jug of cider. "We've earned a break. The stew is on, the next batch of pears is ready to go in the hot water bath and we've plenty of wheat bread left over from yesterday's baking so we don't need to make biscuits for supper."

"You have to tell Leah what you told me and Sara about Magdalena using your mother's bathroom." Ellie eyes were full of mischief as she retrieved two glasses and carried them to the table. "She won't believe it."

Ruby grimaced, accepting the glasses from Ellie. "I hope this doesn't qualify as gossip," she said. "That wouldn't be very charitable to the woman who's going to be my mother-in-law."

"It's not gossip if it happened and you witnessed it," Ellie said, bringing two more glasses over.

Ruby kicked her shoes off and settled into a chair. "Thanks. The cider will hit the spot. It seems to me that this is extra delicious this year."

"Don't change the subject," Leah urged, pouring everyone a glass. "Now that you've dangled this tidbit in front of me, you've got to tell me all."

"All right, you asked for it," Ruby replied, and she launched into the tale of Joseph's mother's *investigation* of the house during their visit. "I actually saw her looking out the window from my aunt's bedroom," she said.

Ellie began to giggle, followed by Leah. Sara tried to keep a straight face but couldn't quite manage it.

Telling it to them was funnier than it had been at the time. "And that's not all," she went on. "When we headed home, I sat in the back of the van so that I could talk to Joseph, but she managed to wedge herself in between us."

"*Between* you? What did you do?" Leah asked.

"What could I do?" Ruby shrugged and took another sip of cider. "She's Joseph's mother. I spent most of the ride looking out the window and listening to her tell him what he should have said to my father and what he should do with his life."

"That woman needs a hobby," Leah quipped, taking another cookie. "If she has time to try to run her grown son's life, she has entirely too much time on her hands."

Ruby rolled her eyes. "What she needs is her own beau."

Ruby met Ellie's gaze and they both burst into laughter.

Sara just smiled, but there was a twinkle

in her dark eyes that made Ruby wonder what she was thinking.

Saturday morning was bright and crisp with the scent of autumn leaves and fresh-cut hay as dozens of friends and neighbors gathered for an old-fashioned haying. Sara's field was a relatively small one, and she, like many others, kept to the traditional ways. The hay had been cut and raked using horsepower, and now many willing hands would join together to pile the drying hay into fragrant stacks and pile them on a wagon for storage in the barn. Most in the neighborhood with larger farms baled their hay, or even had their English neighbors come in with tractors and pack the timothy and clover into huge round bales that could be covered with weatherproof wrap so that it could be left in the field until needed. But with such a small field and so much help, harvesting the loose hay was a reminder of the rich past and all the wisdom that had been passed down from generation to generation.

After the hay was safely stored in the loft to feed the stock through the winter months, the workers and their families would sit down to a big harvest dinner. Sara had organized games for the younger people, and Samuel Mast had brought his team of trained sheep with bells on their harnesses to give the little children rides in a bright green cart with yellow wheels and bells. There would be apple bobbing, corn husking, wood-chopping contests for the men, a pie-tasting event and a few surprise tests of skill. Everyone would eat their fill and end the evening with a singing attended by young and old.

But first, as Sara reminded her guests, there was hay to get in. She'd hitched her team of mules to one hay wagon, and Charley and Miriam had brought another. Usually Miriam liked to drive the horses, but she was in the family way again and Charley wouldn't hear of her climbing on and off a wagon or spending hours in the field. Eagerly, Ruby offered to step in for her. Sara had been a bit dubious, but after the first few minutes, it was obvious to everyone that Ruby Plank was used to handling a team of draft horses.

For Ruby, helping with the haying was much more fun than cooking or setting up the tables for the noonday meal. And it was a beautiful day, cool without being chilly and sunny without a cloud in the sky. Shrieks of running children, barking dogs and mingled voices added to the excitement. Ruby had to guide the team up and down the field at a walk while men and women, their voices joining in "Amazing Grace," forked hay onto the wagon. At times she had to bring the horses to a complete stop, and when they started forward again, she had to take care that they didn't break into a trot. When she reached the fence at the far end, it took some skill to turn the animals and wagon without endangering the growing mound of fragrant hay.

"You're turning that wagon too tight!" Magdalena called to her. Joseph's mother had come out to the edge of the field with another woman to watch, and apparently to offer suggestions from the sidelines.

Ruby laughed and waved. Charley's team of gray Percherons were well trained, the wagon was new and she'd been driving horses for her father since she was ten years old. The hay had been properly stacked by men who knew what they were doing and was in no danger of tumbling off. She felt a lot safer driving across Sara's field with these animals than riding her push-bike on the road with all the motor traffic.

"Better let Joseph drive!" Thomas leaned on his pitchfork and grinned at her.

Ruby paid him no mind. She knew Thomas, Leah's beau, was a tease, especially where girls were concerned. He said something to Joseph; Joseph handed him his pitchfork and came to run alongside the wagon. Ruby's heart filled to the brim and spilled over as she watched him leap up and find his footing. He was so beautiful…so strong. Joseph was everything she'd ever wanted, and she could hardly believe he wanted to marry her.

"I think that's a full load," Joseph said lightly. "Want me to take it back to the barn for you?"

She laughed, looking up at him. "You think I want you to take the reins?"

"I think you're doing just fine," he said, moving to stand behind her. "But maybe you could take up a little slack on right leather." He reached around and covered her hand with his.

"Joseph. What will people think?" She twisted her hand out of his grasp. Her fingers tingled from his touch, and she could feel the joy bubbling up inside. This was the best day, and she was having a wonderful time.

He laughed. "They might think I was giving you some help with the team. They're pretty powerful animals. We wouldn't want a runaway hay wagon, would we?"

"And we wouldn't want to give your mother an excuse to say we were acting inappropriately either." She smiled over her shoulder at him. Just then, the left front wheel rolled over a bump and Ruby lost her balance. For just a second, she struggled to regain her stance, and he steadied her shoulder. She reined the horses a little to the right and the floor of the wagon leveled out.

"Nice," Joseph said.

Ruby tried not to feel pride for the good job she'd done with an unfamiliar team. She might be less than perfect with a needle, but this she could do. It made her feel good to be a vital part of the haying and even better that Joseph was pleased enough with her that he'd dare impropriety to put his arms around her in public.

"As for my mother, maybe I don't care what she thinks," he said.

Ruby didn't respond. Her feelings on that were mixed. She understood that he loved his mother and had to show her respect, but sometimes she wondered if this was something they could work out between them. Magdalena was proving to be a tougher nut to crack than she'd expected.

The second hay wagon, pulled by the mules, passed them going in the opposite direction. Jakob, the blacksmith in the community, had replaced Ellie as driver on the last trip to the barn. Jakob waved and Ruby waved back at him. One of Samuel Mast's twins was standing in the back of the wagon, forking hay into the center, but he was concentrating on his task and didn't look up.

"You think Ellie has her eye on Jakob?" Joseph asked Ruby.

"She wants nothing to do with him." Jakob

was a little person like Ellie, and it was no secret to anyone under Sara's roof that he was definitely interested in courting Seven Poplars's schoolteacher, but, despite his popularity in the community, Ellie seemed immune to his charms. "I think Ellie likes being single."

"I'm glad you don't," he said. "You're sure you don't want help with the team?"

"*Ne*, I'm doing fine on my own."

"Guess who I ran into on the way here this morning?" Joseph asked, but didn't wait for an answer. "Our bishop. He asked me if I was going to need his services this fall. He's said that if we want to be married before Christmas, we'll have to let him know soon because his Thursdays are filling up. He said he had to have a few weeks' notice to call the *banns*, so we really should—"

"Joseph Brenneman!" She reined the Percherons to an abrupt halt, nearly sending Joseph head over teacups. "You talked to your bishop about our wedding without asking me first?" she asked him.

"I told you I was going to."

"I know, but…" She looked up at him. "Are you absolutely positive you want to go through with this? You don't care that I'm a klutz and a terrible cook, not to mention—"

"Hush," he said, grinning at her in a way that

made her knees go weak. "I don't want to hear it. I don't care if you spill the cream and sour the butter and make pancakes like Frisbees. None of that matters to me. From the first day I met you, you never tried to hide your faults. Honesty and caring for each other are what's important to me in a marriage. That's all we need, isn't it?"

Dumbly, she nodded. Should she tell him the truth now? Here in the middle of the hay field? She hesitated for only a moment, but then the chance was lost because Charley was striding through the hay stubble toward the wagon.

"Something wrong?" he called. "That left front wheel isn't loose, is it?"

"Ne," Joseph shouted back. "We're good." He looked down at her, smiling. "We're great, aren't we, Ruby?"

She nodded, a lump in her throat. *"Ya*, great," she agreed.

Chapter Eleven

Joseph waited patiently as Ruby settled two toddlers into a single seat in a little sheep wagon, and then, when she nodded to him, led the wooly team on the path around Sara's hospitality barn. Ruby walked beside the wagon, watching over her two charges, a girl and a boy.

Ruby was good with children. They liked her and took to her quickly, even when she was a stranger. And it was easy to see that she adored them. She was patient and kind. That made Joseph happy, because he knew that Ruby would make a wonderful mother. He could imagine her with their own children. That thought made him smile. All he'd ever wanted was going to be his: a home, a loving wife and children to care for and bring up in the faith. His mother had always said that he had to choose someone who shared his values, a woman he could trust who would put family first, ahead of her own wishes. And he'd done just that.

Ruby glanced up at Joseph and smiled, and his pulse raced. He smiled back at her and wondered why his mother couldn't see what a treasure Ruby was. Couldn't his mother realize that just being near Ruby filled his heart with laughter? When he was with her, he felt a foot taller and able to face any obstacle. If this was what people meant when they joked about being struck by the love thunderbolt, then so be it. He was content to be stricken. The fact that the two most important people in the world to him bristled like grumpy hens when they were together was the only gray cloud on his horizon.

But now wasn't the time to dwell on what had to be resolved. It was time to relax and have some fun. After the hay was all in, he and the other men who'd worked in the field had ducked into the shower at Sara's bachelors' quarters to wash away the results of hard labor. Sara had insisted they all bring a change of clothing. "Can't have you smelling like a barnyard," she'd told them plainly.

Joseph's mother had thought that a little foolish. "What's wrong with a man smelling like good, honest work?" she'd said. "I was never so fancy that I would find fault in your father when he came in from plowing." Joseph had only smiled. But he'd been more than rewarded for his trouble when he'd returned to the yard to find Ruby waiting for him in a fresh, sky blue dress, navy apron and crisp, white *kapp*. She was so pretty that he could feel his throat tighten. God must have sent Ruby to him, because otherwise, he never would have had a chance with her.

Traditionally, men sat together for the communal harvest meal and the women served. Sara didn't try to alter that practice, but once the men had finished and the tables cleared and reset for the women and children, she suggested that the men take a turn at serving. It might not have been what they were accustomed to, but every one, including the Seven Poplars bishop, fell to it with good humor. And after the meal, it was the men who gathered and washed the dishes, the only exceptions being those too old or infirm to take part.

Then the games had begun. Joseph and Ruby had teamed up in the egg-and-spoon race where they'd not done so well because she kept dropping her egg. In the three-legged race, they'd come in a tie for second with Leah and Thomas. They'd helped out with musical chairs, a game played with clapping rather than instruments, and been soundly beaten in several rounds of corn hole. It was clear to Joseph that he had his work cut out for him in teaching Ruby how to toss the bean bags, because she was terrible. But it didn't matter, because she even made finishing last fun.

After the games, they'd found a quiet corner of the yard and shared a slice of lemon-meringue pie, followed up by one of raisin and one of apple cranberry. They'd talked and talked. He was never at a loss for words when he was with her. And even if he couldn't think of something to say, sitting in comfortable silence with Ruby suited him just fine. When they couldn't hold another bite of dessert, the two of them had wandered over to the horseshoe pits and watched Thomas taking on all comers, until Sara had called Ruby to help the little children with the sheep-cart rides. Honestly, he didn't care where they went, what they ate or what they did, so long as he could be with Ruby. Just being near her made him want to shout for joy.

"I like your friends and neighbors," Ruby said to him as they made their way back to the starting point so the children next in line could have a chance to ride in the cart. "They're so welcoming."

"And why wouldn't they be?" he replied shyly. "You're easy to like."

"I hope so. My mother was afraid I'd be

homesick. I've never been away from *Mommi* and *Daddi* before. Does that make me sound immature?"

"Ne." He smiled at her again. "It shows you love your family, which is as it should be."

They returned the children to their waiting grandmothers and then stepped aside to let another set of volunteers take their places with the cart. "Thirsty?" Joseph asked. "I think I could go for some of Anna Mast's lemonade. She freezes slices of lemon rind into the ice and makes her drink tart, the way I like it."

"Sounds good," Ruby agreed. They started walking toward the refreshment tables when Sara approached.

"Having fun?" Sara asked.

"We are." Ruby looked up at Joseph and smiled.

"I have something that I need to discuss with Joseph," Sara explained. "Maybe you could help pour drinks for a few minutes, Ruby, while Joseph and I talk in private?"

Ruby glanced at him again. "Of course," she replied.

"If it concerns me, it concerns Ruby too," Joseph protested. "There's no need for her to leave us."

Sara pursed her lips. "It's about your mother."

"Mother?" He frowned. "And us?"

Sara shook her head. *"Ne,* nothing to do with

you and Ruby, although it might affect you in the future." She looked around. "We'd better go into the house. This isn't something for public knowledge, at least not yet."

"Maybe I should just let the two of you—" Ruby began, but he tucked her arm in his.

"I want you with me," he said.

Ruby nodded and followed him and Sara inside to Sara's office.

"Close the door." Sara waved them to seats in front of her desk and settled into her chair behind it. "I like to keep my matchmaking confidential."

Joseph leaned forward, suddenly very curious. Had she just said *matchmaking*?

"I'll be frank, Joseph. Elmer Raber came to see me in hopes that I could arrange a marriage for him." She folded her hands on her desk. "He's interested in your mother."

Joseph was so stunned that it took him a moment to respond.

Ruby gave a little squeak of surprise.

"My—my mother?" he managed when he found his voice.

Sara chuckled. "Don't look so shocked. Magdalena is still of marrying age. I've negotiated marriages for couples in their eighties. Being alone isn't natural for a man nor a woman." She leaned forward on her desk. "So tell me, what do you think of Elmer? He's financially sound and in good standing with his church. Marrying him would be an advantageous match for your mother. Do you think she'd look favorably on the proposition? I know she's turned down several suitors over the years, but now that you're marrying, perhaps she'd look at the idea in a new light."

Joseph sat back in the chair. He wouldn't have been more surprised if Sara had called him in to make a match for his milk cow. "You're certain it's *my* mother he's interested in? Not some other Magdalena?"

"Joseph." Ruby laid a hand gently on his wrist. "Your mother is still a very attractive woman."

"Exactly." Sara smiled at Ruby. "Attractive, industrious and a credit to the neighborhood. Who cooks *schmitz un knepp* like Magdalena? Or sews such a neat seam?" She picked up a pencil and tapped the point lightly against a yellow legal pad. "Normally, I wouldn't consult a son about his mother's match. But I know how close the two of you are. And you *are* the head of the household." She looked at him, obviously waiting for an answer. When he didn't say anything, she went on. "Do you think she likes Elmer? It's common knowledge that they're friendly, but have you seen any sign that she might feel more for him?"

It hadn't occurred to Joseph that his mother would ever want to marry again. She had always said that she didn't want to bring a stepfather into the house to rule over him. But maybe Sara was right. Now that he had someone of his own, maybe his mother… He removed his hat and balanced it on his knee. It was a lot to think about. Elmer Raber was a good man, and his mother *did* seem to like his company. Hadn't she invited him to supper? Maybe he'd been so concentrated on courting Ruby that he hadn't noticed what was happening in his own house.

"I'll tell you the truth." Sara rocked back in her chair. "When Elmer sent a boy to tell me that he wanted to meet, I thought it was Ruby he was interested in."

Ruby's eyes widened in surprise. "Me?"

Sara chuckled. "*Ach*, if I had a dollar for every person in the last two weeks who told me that Elmer liked Ruby and hoped to win her away from Joseph, well, that would be nice. But when I tracked down the rumor, I discovered it originated from one source. And that wasn't Elmer."

"Who was it?" Ruby asked. "Oh! Did Magdalena tell you that?"

Sara shook her head. "I do not repeat gossip. Not unless I know that the knowledge would do a great deal more good than evil, and that I absolutely know the information to be fact. In any case, it doesn't matter where the rumor started. It's not true. I asked Elmer right out. He made it clear that he thought you were a lovely girl and perfect for Joseph, but that his hopes were set on Joseph's mother. He believes that they are well matched, of an age to be sensible and young enough to look forward to many contented years."

Joseph frowned, trying to wrap his head around what the matchmaker had just said. "I can't think that my mother would start a rumor about Elmer and Ruby. She knows I intend to marry her." He glanced at Ruby. "And it hurts me that you'd assume that of her."

"I'm sorry," Ruby said with a shrug and an apologetic smile. "It just popped into my head."

"And out of your mouth." Sara shook her head. "Young people. You, Ruby, should learn to think before you speak. And you, Joseph," she said turning her attention back to him, "should realize that your mother is having a difficult time accepting your leaving the nest. It's not necessarily a fault—it only proves how much she loves you. Change isn't something that comes easy to us older folk."

"I suppose you're right," he agreed.

"So do you have objections to Elmer?" she pressed. "For your mother, not your betrothed."

He couldn't resist a smile. "*Ne*, so long as it's what she wants."

"Good." Sara slapped her hand on the desk. "That's what I wanted to hear. Your mother deserves a life and a house of her own. She needs someone to take care of, someone other than a son. I was afraid that you might oppose the match. If you did, I'm sure Magdalena would balk at the whole idea. But if you see it as a good thing, then I think your mother will be more open herself to the notion of being courted."

"How can I help?" Joseph asked.

"Just be supportive. I'll arrange a supper and invite them both. And I'd like you and Ruby to be here. I'd like to get you all together and see how it goes. We'll go from there. Agreed?"

Joseph hesitated. "So…do you want me to say something to Mother?"

"*Ne*. Elmer's not quite ready, though I think he will be soon enough. He just wanted me to see how you felt about the idea."

Joseph glanced at Ruby. She was beaming.

He turned back to Sara. "I—I think it's a great idea, and Ruby and I will do anything we can to help."

His mind was already rushing ahead to the possibilities. If his mother married Elmer, she could move into Elmer's house, two church districts away. As Sara had said, marriage would give his mother something else to focus on, which would give him and Ruby time and privacy to settle into their new marriage. It might be the answer to his biggest problem. *"Ya,"* he said, breaking into a grin. "That sounds like a plan."

The following Friday, Joseph, Magdalena, Elmer and Ruby enjoyed a tasty supper at the matchmaker's house. So far, the evening had gone better than anyone could have expected. Magdalena seemed on her best behavior, and Elmer, smiling and witty, had actually gotten and held her attention. Sara's pot roast had been excellent, and Ruby and Joseph had eaten more *kartoffel kleesse* and corn bread than she suspected was wise, even if they did go easy on the green beans with bacon and the slaw.

Sara had Ruby and Joseph help themselves to fat squares of gingerbread heaped with whipped cream and go out on the porch where they could enjoy the mild October weather. Dusk was settling over the house and farmyard, the autumn air smelled of apples and hay, and crickets were keeping up a merry chorus. Ruby loved this time of the day, and she loved this season. It had always been her favorite, and this year she could share it all with Joseph.

"It's a *goot* thing you can't cook like that," he teased as they carried their dessert outside. "I'd soon be too fat to climb the hay ladder."

Ruby chuckled. "I'm not sure if that's a compliment or not, but it's true my cooking skills are limited. I *do* make excellent scrambled eggs though."

"Throw on some cheese and it will do just fine for suppers for me," he answered, taking a seat in one of the chairs on the porch.

She glanced toward the kitchen door and wondered if Sara was telling Magdalena about Elmer's offer of marriage. They'd heard no screaming or crash of broken china so far. Was it selfish to hope that Joseph's mother would surprise them all and be flattered by Elmer's attention? If she *did* accept the offer, that would leave Joseph's home just for him and Ruby. And that would be wonderful. The idea of beginning their marriage alone in a home appealed to her. Of course someday she'd want to move back to Bee Bonnet to care for her parents as they aged but they had made it clear they didn't expect her to return home anytime soon. She and Joseph would have to work out the details. She just liked the idea that they had options, and the option of some time alone with her husband without his mother or her parents would be more than she could hope for.

Maybe it hadn't been Magdalena who'd been spreading the rumor that Elmer was interested in her. It was wrong to suspect someone without proof, but it would be so like Magdalena. *God forgive me*, she thought. *I promised Joseph that I'd try harder to get his mother to like me, and I'm not living up to that promise if I'm suspecting her of trying to sow discord between us.*

What was it her father always said? "Take the log out of your own eye before you worry about a splinter in someone else's." It wasn't quite the same as the verse the preachers quoted from the Bible, but close and just as wise. And her mother was wont to say that you couldn't change another, only yourself. Needless to say, she had a lot of maturing to do to live up to their standards and learn to be charitable.

Ruby sat down and placed her plate of gingerbread on the small table between them. Seated the way they were, her knee almost touched his.

Joseph's gaze met hers and he smiled. He had such a beautiful smile. Whenever he turned it on her, she could feel her bones turn to butter. She averted her gaze, feeling a little shy, realizing that the time had come to spill the beans. For weeks she'd been worrying about keeping something from him, and all for nothing. He'd be pleased, so maybe it wouldn't be such a bad thing to surprise him. It would be like an unexpected gift.

The long-awaited letter from her parents had arrived on Wednesday and she'd been looking for an opportunity to explain everything to Joseph ever since. "Of course, tell your Joseph about your situation," her mother had written in her beautiful, flowing script. "Your father and I are surprised you waited this long. He has every right to know. Our only stipulation was that you and Sara not reveal your true circumstances until we could all be certain that it wouldn't make a difference to him. We were so disappointed in the Noffsinger boy, and I suspect Jason Zehr's motives were less than *goot* ones, as well. But that's in the past. It's easy to see that Joseph is a fine young man, worthy of being your husband."

Ruby lifted her lashes. "Joseph, I…I need to talk to you about…something." Suddenly, she was nervous, and she had no idea why. This was her Joseph, her betrothed. There was no reason to be nervous with him, not ever.

"Okay." He took a bite of gingerbread.

Ruby nibbled at her bottom lip. How to say this without sounding *hochmiedich*? Pride was considered a sin, but the truth was, her secret was a thing to make a girl feel valued and of worth. "It's nothing bad," she said in a burst of words. "It's a good thing, a wonderful thing. I just…" She stared at her lap.

He chuckled, setting his plate down. "What's going on? Have you learned to sew a straight seam?"

"*Ne*, better than that." She clapped her hands together, looking up at him. "You won't believe it."

"Okay…"

She pressed her lips together and barreled forward. "Remember when we met my parents at their house?"

"Of course, I do." His eyes narrowed.

"Well, that wasn't exactly my father's house," she said. "Well, it was, is…but it…isn't."

"I don't understand."

"It's…" She reached for his hand. "You see, the little house, it's my aunt's house. I mean my aunt lives there. Not *Mommi* and *Daddi*."

He looked confused. "So where *do* they live?"

"In the stone house next door." She grimaced and watched him for his reaction. "The big one."

He sat back. "You're telling me that your parents live in that big house?"

"*Ya.*" She exhaled with relief. "It's a long story. Funny, really." She laughed but it came out half-hearted.

All of a sudden Joseph looked uncomfortable.

He let go of her hand. Embarrassed, she withdrew it and tucked it behind her back.

"I'm listening," he said, his tone stiff.

"You see…both houses belong to my parents. The houses and the farm. And the land."

He was frowning. Joseph rarely frowned. "Your father owns land? How much?" he asked.

"A lot," she admitted. "If you count the smaller farms that he rents out…more than a thousand acres." Again, she grimaced. "I think."

"A *thousand* acres?" Joseph's features tightened and his complexion paled. "So you're saying he's rich and you didn't tell me. *Your father is rich.*"

"Not rich, exactly." She chewed on her lower lip. This wasn't going the way she expected it to, not at all. "But he does have the dairy and a herd of milk cows too."

"Your father is rich," Joseph repeated. "What else haven't you told me?"

"That's all." She opened her arms. "Well… I don't know what else you want to know. He's got a hog lot too, and sheep and…I don't know. We don't talk about it. I think he has a business or two. Partnerships. I suppose we should count those." She tried to make a joke of it.

Joseph wasn't smiling and suddenly she felt dizzy. Afraid. She stared at him. "I guess this comes as a surprise," she said, her voice dropping to almost a whisper. "To find out that I'm going to inherit—"

He stood up suddenly. "Ruby, you were untruthful with me! You…you made me think you—" His voice was hard, a tone she'd never heard him use with her before, and the pallor of his face had been replaced with an angry flush of red. "You…you lied to me."

"No, no I never lied," she protested, coming to her feet. "It's just that… Joseph, it's complicated. I had to be certain… My parents and I had to know that you—"

"I think I've heard all I need to," he said abruptly. "You deliberately deceived me."

"*Ne*, I didn't. I mean I did, but—" She exhaled and started again. "Joseph, let me explain." She grabbed his arm, forcing him to look at her. "See…two different boys tried to marry me for *Daddi*'s money. They said they loved me, but they didn't. It was just *Daddi*'s money they wanted. So my parents wanted to make sure that didn't happen again. That's why they sent me here to Delaware. So…no one would try to take advantage of *Daddi*'s—what *Daddi* has."

"And you think I'm like that?" he demanded. "You think I would do something like that?"

"*Ne*, of course not." She looked up at him, but he refused to meet her gaze. She let go of his arm. "You're different, Joseph."

"And so are you, Ruby." He pressed his hands stiffly to his sides. "You—you're not the woman I thought you were. The woman I trusted."

"Joseph, you don't understand." She took a step toward him. "Don't you see, this… It's not a bad thing."

He shook his head. "I can't believe you'd deceive me this way, Ruby. I suppose Sara was in on it too. And who else? Leah? Ellie?"

"Joseph, please."

"I've heard all I want to hear from you today." He turned away from her and strode toward the kitchen door, his shoulders rigid. "Mother," he called sharply. "Let's go. We're leaving."

"What's wrong with you, Joseph?" Magdalena said from inside. "I'm not done with my pie."

"There's pie at home." He stepped inside the door to the house and took her dress bonnet down from the hook on the kitchen wall. He held it out to her.

Magdalena rose from the table, coming to him.

"Let's go," Joseph repeated, handing her the bonnet. "We're going home." Then he turned and went back out the door.

"Joseph," Ruby pleaded as he strode past her on the porch without stopping. "Don't go."

Stunned, she watched with tear-filled eyes as he went down the steps.

"I don't know what's gotten into the boy," his mother fussed from the kitchen door as she tied her bonnet. "I never taught him to be rude. And such a lovely supper, Sara. I can't thank you enough." She opened the door and then turned back. "We'll be expecting you for dinner on Monday, Elmer!"

Chapter Twelve

The day of his cousin Violet's wedding, Joseph arrived at his aunt and uncle's house at seven in the morning. Normally on a Thursday, he'd be working and, considering what had recently happened to his own dreams for marriage, a wedding was the last place he wanted to be. But family had to come first, regardless of his own feelings.

Outsiders might believe that Amish life was one of dour sacrifice, a rigid code of behavior and unrewarding toil. That was as far from Joseph's experience as the moon. Family, worship, community and work filled his world and he loved every hour of it. If it were not for his unwavering faith in God and in the Amish path to salvation, he didn't know if he would have been strong enough to survive losing the woman he'd waited a lifetime to find. *Gelassenheit*. It was what was expected of him and what he must give. He must put his future in the Lord's hands and accept whatever came with as much grace as possible.

Joseph hadn't spoken more than a few words to Ruby since he'd left Sara's home the night of her supper two weeks ago, and only then to tell her he wasn't going to talk about what had happened. She'd come to him, apologizing, trying to get him to talk to her. But what was the point? The engagement was over.

Of course there wasn't an hour that had gone by that he hadn't thought about Ruby or a night that he hadn't lain awake tossing until the first rays of dawn. The previous night had been particularly bad. He'd barely slept a wink, going over and over in his mind what had gone wrong between him and Ruby and thinking about his cousin's coming nuptials. He prayed fervently that the match Sara had made for Violet and John Abbott was better than his own. He hoped they knew each other better than he'd obviously known Ruby.

Despite his mother's vigorous resistance to his betrothal, Joseph had never doubted Ruby. Not only was she beautiful, but he'd believed her to be completely honest, a trait he admired above all else. He'd believed Ruby respected him as a man and the future father of her children. But, apparently, he'd been badly mistaken. Ruby's confession had hurt him so badly that at first he'd been stunned, too numb to feel the pain. But that had soon been replaced by anger, and then by an empty ache that was impossible to shake off. He just couldn't get past the fact that his Ruby, his beloved Ruby, had deceived him.

Another two buggies pulled into the leaf-strewn yard and Joseph moved to take the bridle of the nearest horse. "Go on inside," he said to the couple. It was almost ten and the services would soon begin. "I'll tend to your horse." After the family got out of the second buggy, Joseph waved to the driver to follow him to a line of horses and buggies tied to a board fence on the far side of the barn.

Joseph's aunt and uncle were well liked in the neighborhood and the wedding would be well attended. Groups of men stood near the well, the shed and the windmill. They were talking crops, weather and the availability of fertile land for sale in upper New York State and western Virginia while the women gathered inside to exchange the latest news and help with the preparation of the meals.

Sara, Ruby and Leah had arrived early, as well, to help with the dinner preparations, but Joseph had stood back and allowed Andy to take charge of their buggy. Ruby had seen him when she'd gotten down from the vehicle, but had wisely averted her gaze and continued on inside without attempting to speak to him. If she had tried, he didn't know what he would have done. Walked away? He wasn't discussing their breakup; there was no point. And he wasn't ready to talk to her about the weather or what was being served for the wedding dinner with her. He didn't know when or if he'd ever be.

A few laughing children, dressed in their black Sunday best, came out the back door and proceeded to chase one another around the yard. Joseph assumed that they belonged to guests who'd traveled to attend, probably the bridegroom's relatives from Ohio. Local mothers had come with a few babies and toddlers, but fewer kids were present than would be at other Amish gatherings. Most youngsters were at school or at home today under the watchful eye of babysitters because weddings were usually adult affairs. There would be a morning sermon, the seated midday dinner and another worship service in the afternoon before the evening supper.

Some families would stay for the entire event, while others had been invited for one meal or the other. No matter what the hour, the food would be fantastic and plentiful, and the services long and serious. A marriage wasn't simply the joining of a man and a woman, but a joyous addition to the families, faith and community. This was the first of what would be a full wedding season for the Amish of Kent County. Although weddings were traditionally held in November, after harvest, Violet and John's was being held in October, due to the large number of marriage ceremonies scheduled this autumn.

Normally the wedding ceremony and morning services would be held at another home nearby while the bride's parents' house was prepared for the wedding dinner with the elaborate arrangement of table setups and the *Eck*, the traditional corner of the main room where the bride and groom and their attendants sat. But Violet's parents' house was a large one, and they'd decided to have the sermon and the exchange of vows here. It would require a quick change of seating and place setting to make the change from worship service to wedding feast, but there were many willing hands to help.

"Joseph! It's time!"

He looked up to see his aunt waving from the back porch. He glanced down the driveway and saw that there were no other arrivals in sight. His thoughts still in turmoil, he crossed the yard amid a flurry of swirling maple leaves in vivid shades of brown, red and gold.

He entered the house to find most of the guests, and the bridal couple, already seated. Both the men's and women's sections were full in the main rooms, and half the chairs were taken into an adjoining chamber that normally served as a guest bedroom.

"Here." Andy waved him to an empty spot in a row of unmarried young men.

Joseph slid in and removed his hat, tucking it under the bench just as one of the elders stood and signaled for the opening wedding hymn. They were halfway through when the preachers and the bishop filed in from an adjoining room and took their chairs in front of the assembly.

Joseph glanced at John and Violet sitting side by side up front. Even though they'd only met a few months ago and spent only a short time together, they seemed content with the match Sara had made for them. John was smiling and Violet was positively radiating joy in her new apron, dress and *kapp*. Watching her and her new husband-to-be, it gave Joseph pause to realize that after today, she would carefully pack her clothing away, not to be worn again until the day of her burial, hopefully many, many years in the future. Violet was so full of life that it was hard to imagine her as an old woman, her plain but cheerful face lined with age.

Two hymns later, the first preacher opened

with a sermon about the sanctity of marriage and the need for a man and wife to stand together, no matter the trials of life. Never must they consider the option of divorce, for marriage was a sacred institution and one entered willingly with loving hearts. Family, he insisted, was the foundation of their faith and vital to God's plan. He went on to speak of the necessity of putting aside self and of honesty in all matters concerning each other.

The words fell like cold rain over Joseph. Honesty. That was what he'd required above all else from his wife-to-be, and true to his mother's prediction, Ruby had been hiding something. It didn't matter that she might have been hurt by other suitors before. She should have trusted him. She should have been truthful. And how could he go into a marriage with her if she didn't think she could be honest with him? Marriage was a sacred union, to be broken only by death. If he made a mistake, he'd have to live with it for the rest of his life, and a house divided by something so important was too weak to survive.

"Joseph." Andy nudged him. "Stand."

He rose quickly, feeling his cheeks flush with embarrassment that others might have noticed he was slow to get to his feet for the next hymn. He didn't need the *Ausbund*; he knew the more familiar hymns by heart. By force of will, he devoted his attention not only to the singing but to the lengthy sermons that followed. This was Violet's day, and he was determined not to do anything that would detract from her happiness.

It was shortly after twelve when the actual marriage ceremony took place. The bishop invited the couple to stand and answer the familiar questions. With his people there was no elaborate wedding clothing, no rings, no music or flowers. Violet and John just promised to be faithful and to support one another in front of God and these witnesses. And when each had uttered the words and clasped hands, the bishop had given his blessing to the union, a blessing echoed in the hearts of the entire community.

There were final words from the bishop and one of the preachers and several more hymns before the service ended. Then everyone, including the bride and groom, hurried to change the seating arrangements and prepare the house for the wedding dinner.

Joseph found himself immediately pressed into service setting up tables and carrying boxes of glassware from a second bench wagon in the yard. As he passed through the kitchen, he caught a glimpse of Ruby and he felt a moment of panic. Their gazes locked, and he forced himself to turn and walk away, head down.

"Joseph?" A hand gripped his forearm and he looked down to see Sara standing in the doorway. "You can't go on avoiding me too," she said quietly.

"I don't want to discuss this with you," he answered. His throat tightened and he felt a stinging behind his eyelids. He stared at the floor, gripping the box of glasses he held. "Not here. Not today."

She exhaled impatiently. "You can't continue to refuse to talk to Ruby. You need to settle this between you, if only so that you can both move on."

He shook his head, glancing up. People were watching. Listening. "Excuse me." He gestured toward the living room. "They're waiting for the glasses."

Sara grabbed his sleeve. "Joseph, Ruby's devastated."

"And you think I'm not?" He shoved the box into another man's arms. "Can you take this in?" Then, leaving Sara standing there, he walked back through the kitchen and out into the crisp midday air.

His chest felt as though a great weight was pressing on it. He hadn't wanted to be rude to Sara, but she'd been part of the deception. Did she think he could just forget that? He needed fresh air. He needed to get away from the smiles and laughter of the wedding celebration.

Shaken, he ducked around the corner of the house and walked away between the rows of corn shocks that marched in neat rows away from the farmyard. A brisk wind had picked up, sending chaff and dust whirling through the air, making it easy for Joseph to tell himself that the liquid that filled his eyes wasn't tears.

"A good wedding," Sara said to Ruby as she guided the driving mule down the dark lane. "A good match. I think they will be very happy together."

It was late, after ten. She and Sara had stayed to clean up after the guests left. They were alone because Leah had ridden home with one of her sisters, where she would spend the night. Ruby was glad that it was only the two of them because she needed to talk to the matchmaker. And, as much as she liked Ellie and Leah, she didn't want any more of their advice.

"You're quiet," Sara said. "Are you tired?"

"A little," Ruby replied. She shivered in the damp night air as goose bumps rose on her arms. She'd worn her green wool dress and cape, but she'd not brought a wrap. Mist rose from the fields to cloud the road and make it difficult to see the road ahead. Sara's buggy had lights and large reflectors, but the fog made the mule's hooves echo eerily off the hard surface of the blacktop. Ruby was glad that they didn't have far to go. It wasn't a good night to be on the road in a buggy.

"I wanted to tell you, Sara, that…that I've decided to go home," she said, swallowing and trying to hold back her tears. "To Bee Bonnet."

Bright headlights poured into the buggy from behind. Sara didn't speak until the car had passed them and vanished into the gray void ahead. A dog barked in the distance, and the alarm was taken up by two more. Ruby hugged her arms tightly against her chest as the first tear escaped and rolled down her cheek, followed by another.

"So you're giving up on Joseph?" Sara made a harrumphing sound. "I thought you were more determined than that."

Ruby sniffed and searched in her pocket for a tissue. "He wouldn't even look at me today."

"Joseph's stubborn, I'll give him that."

"I…I don't know what to do." A sob escaped her and she covered her mouth with her hand. There was no stopping the tears. "I've made… such a mess of things."

A truck passed, coming from the other direction, but the mule paid it no heed. The buggy kept rolling through the darkness. "So that's it? You've giving up and going home?"

"I don't want to give up," Ruby admitted. "But Joseph doesn't want me anymore. He's made that clear."

Sara sighed. "I feel partially responsible for this. I tried to tell your parents that deception is never a practice I recommend for courtship, but I didn't refuse to participate. Trust lost isn't easily regained. But Joseph cares deeply for you. We just have to give him time. I think he'll come around, once he smoothes his ruffled feathers and calms down. It's no small thing for a young man to suddenly discover that the penniless *maedle* he planned to make his wife will be a wealthy woman."

"Not *wealthy*."

Sara scoffed. "*Ya. Rich* by our standards. Do you know the value of Lancaster County farmland? Some say it is the most fertile topsoil in the world. Your father's land is better than gold locked in a vault somewhere."

"The land isn't mine," Ruby argued halfheartedly. "It's *Daddi*'s and *Mommi*'s."

"But in the Lord's time, it will pass to you and eventually to your children, should you be so blessed. As it should be if you and Joseph are good stewards and you live as you should, following the right path that God has planned for you."

The mule pricked up his ears and quickened his stride.

"Sara, you're not listening to me. It's been two weeks." Ruby clasped her hands in her lap. "I've tried to apologize. At least three times, but Joseph doesn't want to hear it. He wouldn't even speak to me today. He's not going to get over this."

"Maybe not, but I'm not ready to give up on the two of you, not yet," Sara said. "What I'm trying to figure out is whether Joseph's problem with you is the fact that you led him to believe you were poor, or that his wife will be financially secure in her own right. Some men find it difficult to accept when a woman is well set up. That's a truth I've learned over the years."

"Joseph's not like that." Ruby sniffed. "We talked about how things would be when we married. What is his will be mine and mine his. He said my opinion on matters would be important to him. He said we would always make decisions together." A sob escaped her lips. "Sara, can't you try to talk to him for me?"

"I tried, but he wasn't any more willing to talk with me than he was with you. Probably less," Sara admitted. She was quiet for a moment and then went on. "But I don't think you should go back to your mother just yet. I still believe the two of you are a solid match. Better than most." She nodded thoughtfully, gripping the reins. "We just need to figure out how to fix this."

"But how are we going to fix it?" Ruby whispered.

"I don't know yet, but if you'll stay, I promise you, I'll think of something."

Ruby took a deep breath. "All right. I'll stay another week, but if we've made no progress, I think I should go home."

"If you have the sense God gave you, you'll stay as long as I tell you to. A man like Joseph doesn't come along every day, and if you leave before it's settled, you may regret it for the rest of your life."

"It's good of you to give up your Saturday evening to chaperone us," Elmer said to Joseph as he pushed back from the kitchen table.

"It's our pleasure." His mother beamed as she refilled Elmer's coffee cup. "And Joseph doesn't mind a bit, do you?"

"Ne," Joseph said. And he didn't, not really. Since he'd stopped seeing Ruby, he hadn't been in the mood to socialize with friends. Andy had been making himself scarce on nights when the

two of them used to go in search of a singing, volleyball game or birthday party.

"*Goot.* I'm afraid I'm making a pest of myself since this is the third time I've shared supper with you and your mother this week." Elmer patted his stomach. "And *goot* suppers they were too."

Joseph nodded, though he'd barely tasted his pork chop and scalloped potatoes.

"You're so quiet that I was afraid you were coming down with something," Elmer went on when Joseph didn't say anything. "You know Harvey Zook from over near Willow Grove has the walking pneumonia. Last Tuesday. Milking cows in the morning and sitting in a hospital bed in Dover by supper."

"You think Joseph is sick?" his mother asked. She came around the table and pressed the back of her hand to his forehead. "He doesn't feel too warm."

Joseph held up his hands in protest. "I'm not sick. I'm fine. Just…I'm fine."

Elmer stirred a lump of sugar into his coffee. "I thought maybe Ruby would be here tonight. Haven't seen her in ages. Have you two set a date yet?"

Joseph exchanged looks with his mother. He hadn't said anything about the breakup, but he'd assumed that she'd told Elmer. Apparently, she hadn't. She corrected that over-sight within seconds.

"Ruby and Joseph aren't seeing each other anymore," his mother explained smoothly. "She'd been keeping a secret from him. I knew there was something. Call me suspicious, but she had Joseph fooled."

"I'm sorry." Elmer grimaced. "I didn't know. I didn't mean to pry."

"*Ne.*" Joseph shook his head. "It's all right."

"Hardly." His mother's brows knitted as she leaned forward eagerly to share the news with Elmer. "She deceived us all. For what reason, we'll never know. But she's not a poor girl like she insinuated. Her father owns a lot of land, and he has many businesses. Ruby is the only child, so she'll inherit it all. You know what everyone would be saying from here to Lancaster County. That Joseph married a plain-faced girl just for her fortune." She pursed her lips and nodded in the satisfied way she did when she'd been proven right. "I think too much of Joseph to have him be thought of that way."

"Ruby's not plain," Joseph protested. "Please stop saying that. She's a beautiful person, inside and out."

"You see what I mean?" his mother interrupted, throwing up her hands. "You see, Elmer? He was so besotted by her that he couldn't see what was right in front of his eyes. I'd not be uncharitable by calling her homely, but—"

"That's enough, Mother," Joseph said quietly. "I won't have you talk that way about Ruby."

His mother got to her feet, snatched a butter dish and her empty coffee cup and marched back across to the sink. Her back was rigid as she busied herself with the dishes. "Sons. When they fix on a girl, they lose all their sense." And then she turned back and looked directly at Elmer. "I'm going to have a good talk with Sara Yoder. What was she thinking? She must have known the truth, and that makes her almost as guilty as Ruby. Sara can make up for it by finding a more suitable bride for Joseph. And this time, I'll be the one to decide if she's suitable before she and my son ever lay eyes on one another."

"Mother, please," Joseph said. He bit back the words that rose in his throat. He couldn't disrespect her, especially in front of the man she hoped to marry. But he wouldn't sit here and listen to this. If Elmer hadn't been there, he would have gotten up and walked out. He didn't want to seem to be having a childish tantrum, but neither could he let her go on about Ruby so.

"It's not my place to interfere in a family affair..." Elmer began.

"*Ne*, say what you have to say. Maybe you

can talk some sense into Joseph. You saw her. Did *you* think she was beautiful?"

Elmer averted his eyes. "I never believed it was fitting for a man my age to talk that way about a young woman, and certainly not one who was betrothed to someone. She seemed a lovely girl to me. Young, of course, but that's what a young man needs."

"I see how it is," she replied. "You men stick together. But—" Joseph's mother shrugged "—I was proved right, wasn't I? There was always something about her that didn't sit right with me." She dropped a bowl into her dishpan and it splashed a tide of water over the edge of the sink and down the front of her dress. *"Ach,"* she cried. She ran her fingers over the soaked cloth. "We'll say no more about her, if it upsets you so, Joseph. Excuse me while I go and change into something dry." She wrung out her dish-cloth, hung it over the faucet and headed out of the kitchen.

Neither he nor Elmer said anything.

His mother paused in the doorway. "I'm sorry if I embarrassed you, son. But you're better-off without her. Anyone can see that. And when Sara finds you a more appropriate match, you'll see it too."

Silence reigned in the kitchen for several minutes after she was gone, and then Elmer drained the last drop of coffee and pushed the cup away. "I can see that Magdalena had strong feelings about your betrothal. You know that I have a lot of respect and admiration for her."

He met Joseph's gaze meaningfully. They hadn't discussed Elmer's talk with the matchmaker, but he knew Joseph knew.

"But I have to tell you," Elmer went on. "I don't agree with her on this. It doesn't look to me as if you're better-off without Ruby. I'd say it's the other way entirely."

Joseph rose and began to pace back and forth. "I do miss her," he admitted after a minute or two. "But I… She really hurt me, Elmer. I feel—feel betrayed. She didn't trust me enough to tell me the truth about her father's worth. She thought I was the kind of person who would pretend to fall in love with her because she'll come into money someday."

"I can see how it would be a shock, learning such a thing about the woman you were going to marry. But think about it for a minute. This isn't a bad thing. Not a bad thing at all. Not like she had behaved inappropriately in the past. Or if she was thinking of leaving the church. That would be worse." Elmer was quiet for a moment and then went on. "Joseph, I know just how difficult it is to find someone you look forward to seeing at the end of the day, someone you can feel comfortable with at evening prayers. I'd hate to see the two of you make a worse mistake by letting something like this divide you. I agree that there shouldn't be secrets between a man and a woman looking to marry, but…I expect Ruby thought she had a good reason."

Joseph sighed. "It was what her parents wanted. Some other boys had courted her just for the money. I guess her parents thought that if no one knew what they had, a boy would see Ruby for who she is."

"So there you go." Elmer sat back in the kitchen chair. "You can see how a father who loved his only child might err on the side of caution."

"My mother said she was suspicious of Ruby from the beginning. She never thought she was the right one for me." Joseph came to stand behind his empty chair and look across the table. "I don't know, Elmer. I don't know what's right. What I should do?"

Elmer smiled at him. "You should pray, Joseph. That's my advice to you. Take it to the bishop or one of the preachers if it seems too heavy a burden. Your mother is a good woman, devoted to her faith and family. You can't fault her for that. But she can't make this decision for you. I certainly can't." He hesitated. "The thing is, I wouldn't want you to lose out on someone you were meant to be with over bruised pride."

Chapter Thirteen

The following morning was bright and crisp, a beautiful fall day, so pleasant that Sara hadn't bothered to have Hiram hitch up the buggy, but had decided to take her scooter to Magdalena's instead. The exercise would do her good, she reasoned, after all the wonderful food she'd eaten at Violet and John's wedding and in anticipation of the wedding season. She loved the festive air of weddings, but she couldn't resist trying other women's biscuits and pies. If she didn't watch what she put in her mouth, she could easily be as plump as Anna Mast.

When Sara reached Magdalena's home, she was a little winded. Pausing to catch her breath and regain her professional composure, she scanned the small, tidy house. The curtains were pushed back at the kitchen window, a good sign that the woman she'd come to call on was present.

What lovely flowers Magdalena grew, Sara thought as she pushed her scooter up the drive. The beds were a riot of fall colors: red and orange zinnias, gold mums, purple monkshood and brown and green ornamental grasses. There was a big clay pot of herbs at the step with basil, oregano and rosemary, still healthy and green. The door was closed, but it would be if Joseph's mother was home alone.

Magdalena responded immediately to Sara's knocking. "Sara?" Magdalena's surprised expression quickly changed to one of welcome. She pushed the door open wide and peered around her to see if anyone was with her. "Come in. I was just thinking of you. I imagine you came on business. But Joseph isn't here. He's at work."

"Actually, it was you I came to see." Sara followed her into a cheerful yellow kitchen. Magdalena kept the neatest kitchen in Seven Poplars; there wasn't a dirty dish in the sink, a cup out of place or a flowerpot that wasn't a mass of blooms.

"Would you like hot tea?" Magdalena went to the gas range and turned on the flame under the teakettle. "I was just thinking I could use a cup of Earl Grey. Unless you'd rather have coffee?"

Sara nodded her head. Common courtesy meant that she couldn't launch into her reason for coming until they had shared a beverage and exchanged news about each other's households. "Tea is fine. I hope I didn't interrupt your work."

"I was just finishing up some baby gowns and a dress for Mattie Ann Troyer's children. What with Ezra being laid up with a broken ankle, money is tight. I thought her little ones could use some warm new clothes for the cooler weather."

"That's kind of you," Sara replied. "My cousin Hannah's sewing circle is going to auction off a quilt to help with the medical expenses."

"I know the family will appreciate it. Doctors come so expensive today, don't they?" Magdalena measured loose tea into a blue teapot. "I see you came on your scooter. It must be four miles. I do admire you, Sara. So energetic for a woman your size." Magdalena brought mugs and a cream pitcher to the table. It was wooden, with a scrubbed white pine finish, obviously old and well cared for. Hanging from the ceiling over the table was a lovely oil lamp that had been fitted for propane. Already on the table were a blue-and-white pottery sugar bowl and a small vase, shaped like a woven basket, filled with tiny yellow mums. "I thought we should have a talk about Joseph," she said. "Straighten out this whole mess and start over with a different—"

"My first concern today is you, Magdalena."
Sara smiled at her.

"Me?" The teakettle whistled and Magdalena
went to the stove to pour hot water into the teapot.

"I'll get to the point. Women our age don't
have time to pussyfoot around." Sara folded her
hands, resting them on the table. "Elmer Raber
has made a request for a formal offer of marriage. To you," she added.

Magdalena was just putting the lid on the teapot. She dropped it and it rattled on the counter,
but it didn't break. "He wants to... Did you say
'offer of marriage'?" she sputtered.

"I sure did. Now, Elmer understands you've
been an independent woman for many years,
taken care of your own finances. For that reason, he's willing to settle a nice little nest egg on
you, payable at the time of the wedding." She removed a slip of paper from her dress pocket and
slid it across the table to Joseph's mother. "This
full amount will be deposited to your bank account if you agree."

Magdalena's eyes widened as she stared at the
piece of paper on the table. Her lips parted, but
for once, she didn't seem to be able to speak. Finally, she inhaled and stammered. "Elmer wants
to give me..." She picked up a paper fan from

the table and began to fan herself rapidly. "He wants to give me money to marry him?"

"Well, not exactly to marry him. He wants you to marry him because he thinks the two of you would get on well together." Sara rose from her chair and went to retrieve the teapot, securing its lid as she walked back across the kitchen toward the table. "It's not unknown in other parts of the country. In other Amish communities. It's a sign of good will, so that you know you'll be well provided for and not be totally dependent on your new husband." She sat down and poured them both tea. "Furthermore, if and when you do marry, he'll put your name on everything he owns, share and share alike."

Magdalena gripped the back of her chair with one hand while fanning herself with the other. There was a bright spot of red on each of her cheeks. "I...I don't know what to say. Elmer wants to marry *me*?"

"He does. He tells me he respects and admires you, and enjoys your company. He hopes that you will consider him as a suitor with the object of holy matrimony, if and when you find it agreeable." Sara chuckled. "Those were his very words to me, and quite a mouthful for Elmer, I must say."

"Ach." Magdalena covered her mouth with slender fingers. "I thought... That is, I *hoped*

he wasn't just coming for my pot roast, but..."
She looked at Sara. "It's quite amazing, isn't
it? That Elmer would think so highly of me?"

"And why wouldn't he? Now, sit and have
your tea." She began pouring. "You're still a
young and vibrant woman. No one makes better cakes, and you sew like a tailor. You are a
fine catch, Magdalena. You look years younger
than you are, and God has blessed you with
good health. Why wouldn't Elmer want to
marry you?" She slid Magdalena's cup across
the table to her. "The question is, are you interested in Elmer? I know you've turned down
other offers."

She nodded, slipping into her chair. "I have,
but not for years. When Joseph was younger, I
was reluctant to give over his welfare to a stepfather. Joseph and I always had a special relationship, and I was content to raise him myself.
But now..." She fluttered the fan faster. "I don't
know what to say."

Sara took a sip of the tea. It was good, fresh
and sweet on her tongue. "Your son is a grown
man. It's time for him to marry and become
the head of his own family. It's not too late for
you to enter a new relationship. Now, tell me,
do you like Elmer?"

"I...I do," Magdalena admitted. "He's hardworking and soft-spoken. And he seems easy

to please at the dinner table. The bishop speaks well of him. They are distantly related. But… this is all so sudden." She looked down at her tea and then up at Sara again. "Does he want an immediate answer?"

"Of course not. Elmer wants you to take as much time as you need. He did say that he hoped I'd be able to tell him that it's not out of the question, that you will consider his offer." When Magdalena didn't answer, Sara said pointedly, "So, will you consider his offer?"

"I—I'll have to speak with Joseph. This isn't a good time for him. He might want me to be here with him."

"I've already broached the subject with Joseph, and he thinks it's a wonderful idea."

"He does?" Magdalena nodded. "Well, I… I'll have to think…to pray on it. It's a big decision."

"It is." Sara smiled at her again. "So I can tell Elmer that he may hope?"

"*Ya*, he can." A blush tinted her cheeks. She set down the fan, then picked it up and began to fan herself again. "My goodness, what a morning. I didn't expect this."

Sara looked at her. "What did you think? How many times has Elmer been at your table recently? Attended your church services? Surely you didn't think that all those meetings were coincidence, did you?"

She let out a pent-up breath. "*Ne*, but I wasn't sure. I didn't want to get my hopes up and look foolish, so I told myself that he was just lonely and looking for friendship."

"He *is* looking for friendship. But also more."

Magdalena pressed her lips together, seeming to fight a smile. "I always thought that I'd remain single. Joseph's father and I had a good marriage, but he's been gone for many years. I've gotten used to doing things my own way."

"I understand perfectly." Sara picked up her mug. "But there are advantages for a woman with grown children to marry again." She glanced around the kitchen. "Once Joseph takes a wife, you'd have to share this home with her. And in time, it will be her kitchen and, God willing, her children's. I'm sure you'll always have a place here, but it won't be the same place it has been. A mother must come second to a wife."

"I never wanted to be alone," Magdalena admitted. "To come home to an empty house."

"Exactly. And in a second marriage, you would be mistress of the house. You and Elmer would have many years of active living ahead of you. This way you can visit with your son and go home to your own domain whenever the grandchildren get too loud. Elmer likes to travel. He has relatives all over the country, and he told me that if you married, he'd take you anywhere you'd like to go for a honeymoon. He's lonely too. I've made inquiries of his late wife's friends and family. It's something I do. And they have only the best to say of Elmer. If anything, his sisters-in-law say he's too easygoing and tended to let his wife make most of the family decisions. He stands in good stead with his church community, he's charitable and I've seen his financial statements. You'd be hard put to do better."

Magdalena reached for her mug. "I'll think on it," she agreed.

"Good. I will warn you though." She sipped her tea. "Another widow's family has already approached me asking questions about Elmer. If you refuse him, someone else wants me to arrange a match with him."

"Who? Is it Mary Jane Byler? She's sixty-five if she's a day. And old in her ways."

Sara tried not to laugh. There was no dust gathering on Magdalena's *kapp*. "I'm not at liberty to say who. Just that Elmer has other options."

She tugged at an imaginary loose strand of hair and tucked it over her left ear. "But he chose me."

"He did. Elmer thinks you're very attractive. And he says he's never tasted better gravy."

"Well, fancy that. A beau at my age." Magdalena beamed. "I'm not agreeing just yet, of course. I'll have to pray on it."

"That's always best. And you can speak to the elders on the matter. Their wisdom never fails."

"True, true." Magdalena held her mug between her hands and looked across the table at Sara. "Thank you so much for…" She glanced away. "Thank you."

"You're most welcome." Sara gave a nod, thinking that, while Magdalena could be offputting at times, she truly was good woman. "Now, while I'm here, we might as well talk about Joseph."

"Goot." Magdalena set down her mug. "I do hope you have other girls in mind for him. This time, I'd like to appraise them before you introduce anyone to Joseph."

"Ne. I wanted to speak to you about Joseph and Ruby," Sara said firmly.

"That's over." She pursed her lips. "It's clear she isn't the one for him."

"Magdalena," Sara said, taking care with her words. "No one is more devoted to a son than you are to Joseph. And I know that, in your heart, you want his happiness."

"It's all I've ever wanted. To teach him to walk in God's grace, to follow our teachings and to be happy."

Sara fixed her with a knowing look. "Then you know he's unhappy without Ruby. And if he persists in this stubborn behavior, she'll return to her parents and eventually find someone else."

"I think it's best if she goes home." Magdalena sniffed. "Joseph will find a more suitable wife, someone that I can get along with."

"A girl you can get along with or one that will make Joseph happy?" Sara paused and then went on. "You loved your husband. And even if you decide to marry Elmer, it will never be like that first love. It will be different, good, satisfying, but not the passion of young love. Am I right?"

Magdalena frowned, not meeting Sara's gaze. "I suppose you're right."

"Here's my question to you. What if Joseph never finds someone he loves as much as he loves Ruby? What if he never marries and never has children for you to bounce on your knee? Have you considered that in years to come, he may blame you for the breakup?"

"Me?" Magdalena's drew herself up. "Why would Joseph blame *me*? Ruby's the one who deceived him about her financial situation."

"True. But then she told him the truth. And she's apologized to him for not telling him sooner. And tried to talk to him, but Joseph will have no part of a discussion." Sara sat back in her chair. "Honestly, Magdalena, I've been surprised by his behavior. Not being willing to talk over differences is not very mature. And it's not the Amish way. Doesn't our Bible teach us forgiveness and compassion?"

Magdalena looked down at her hands, folded on the table. "*Ya*, it does."

"And tell me, how much of your opposition to Ruby has instigated this? How much have you influenced him in his decision to back out of this courtship?"

"That's silly." Magdalena got to her feet, her face flushed again, this time with distress. "I'm the one who sent Joseph to you. I *wanted* him to find a wife."

"*Ya*, you did. But is it possible that you never expected a woman to fall in love with your son and him with her? Did you think that an arranged marriage would be one of convenience? And that way, you would remain first in your son's heart?"

"That's a terrible thing to accuse me of," Magdalena said. She picked up a dish towel, then set it down on the counter again. "Do you think I'm that selfish?"

"I think you are a good mother and a good woman who may have judged a girl too harshly because you were afraid that she would take your only child from you. And I think that when your son reacted badly, you didn't give him a piece of your mind." Sara rose to her feet. "You are a strong person, Magdalena, and I know you have a loving heart. I only ask that you consider if Joseph's breaking off this courtship with Ruby is better for Joseph—or for you."

"Did he tell you that?" Now Magdalena looked hurt. "Is that what my son thinks?"

Sara shook her head. "No, he didn't say that. I think he's hurt and maybe a little confused. So hurt and confused that he doesn't know what to think."

"You want me to talk to him. Is that what you're asking me to do?"

"I'm asking you to consider what I've told you. I'm asking you to pray for guidance and do what is best for all of you, especially your son. Because if you can bring the two of them back together and she is what will make him happy, he'll thank you for it for the rest of his life."

Joseph scooped mortar on his trowel and slapped it on a concrete block. He was working on the third row of a foundation addition to Moses King's house. He used the trowel edge to smooth and tidy up the wet mix and then added the next block to the row. He settled the block in place and eyed the string line to be certain he was laying a straight course. Turning back to the board, he shaped and turned over the mortar, mentally gauging the amount of moisture in the mix. It was just right. Too much water in the mortar would make a weak wall, and too little would make it difficult to work.

"Joseph!" James called to him. "Your mother's here to see you!"

Joseph laid down his trowel and climbed out of the foundation. His mother? What could be wrong that she'd come to his worksite? He noticed that James was grinning and realized that if his mother hadn't come for an urgent reason, he'd face teasing from his friends and fellow workers. Striding toward his mother's horse and wagon, he tugged off his concrete-smeared leather gloves. He dropped them on a stack of concrete blocks as he passed them.

"Is something wrong?" he asked as he approached the wagon.

She was climbing down. She was wearing her black church dress and her bonnet, full apron and cape. He was immediately perplexed. She hadn't mentioned needing to go into Dover for anything, and she rarely drove herself, claiming that traffic made her uneasy on the road.

"*Ya*, plenty is wrong," she said.

He stared at her. She was definitely giving mixed messages. She'd said there was a problem, but she didn't appear as if she was sick or the house was on fire or someone they knew was in the hospital. And she seemed calm. He'd told her that he was coming home for the midday meal, so what was so important that she couldn't wait? He glanced over his shoulder and saw that James and Amos had both stopped putting up cedar shakes on the main house and were watching.

"Where are you going?" he asked, torn between concern for her welfare and embarrassment that she'd interrupted his work. Once mortar was mixed, you had to use it or throw it away. He didn't have time to waste, but he couldn't fail to show respect for his mother in front of the work crew.

"I'm coming *here*." She looked back at the horse. "You should take her out more often, you know. She doesn't stand to be harnessed very well. I had a time hitching her up. And I think the left back wheel on this wagon is loose. It squeaks. Your father wouldn't approve. You know how careful he was with his equipment. A little grease saves—"

"Mother?" he said sharply, cutting off her lecture on the benefits of maintenance of farm vehicles, which he knew from experience could be quite lengthy. "I'm working. If nothing's wrong, what do you need?"

She turned back to him. "I've made a mistake."

"What are you talking about?" He took her arm and tried to steer her back to the wagon, but she planted her feet and wouldn't be moved.

"I just told you. I've made a terrible mistake." She hesitated. "About Ruby."

He stared at her.

"*Ya*, I admit it. I was wrong. I've thought about it and—" Her eyes suddenly filled with tears. "I didn't mean to interfere. You know I've always wanted what was best for you. I always—"

"Mother, better we talk about this at home." He threw another look back at James and Amos. They were talking to each other, and he didn't doubt that it was about him. "I'll be home in an hour. You go home now, and I'll be along soon."

"*Ne*." His mother raised a finger and shook it at him. "*Ne*. Now. I'll talk to you now and you'll listen." She sniffed and blinked. A tear escaped and trickled down her cheek and she brushed it away "Even though I know it's time for you to marry, maybe a part of me wanted to keep things the way they are. Just you and me. I never thought I was a jealous person, but I think maybe in this, I was."

"Mother, this isn't the time for such a conversation," he protested. Again, he tried to take her arm, but she pulled away from him.

"Joseph, you'll hear me out here and now because…because, maybe in an hour, I won't have the courage to say these things to you. Maybe I'll have second thoughts, and the jealousy will creep back in."

He glanced over his shoulder again and then at her. "Please, keep your voice down. I don't want James to hear you."

She brushed away his concerns with a careless gesture. "James is a good man. Surely, he understands that sometimes there are things only a mother can say to her son? That family matters are more important than concrete blocks? This is important, and you will hear me out."

"Mother, private matters are not for everyone to hear."

"And you think this is a secret that I didn't approve of your Ruby? That I didn't find fault with her when she tried to win my approval? Half of Kent County knows that I was pleased when you fell out with your Pennsylvania girl. And I am ashamed of my behavior. And of yours," she added.

"Mine?"

"You're behaving childishly. You and Ruby have had an argument and—"

"It was more than an argument, Mother. She—"

"And you won't interrupt me." Again, she

held up her finger. "That girl came to you and tried to apologize. I heard the two of you on the front porch last week."

"You were listening in?" he demanded.

"That's not the point. The point is that she made a poor choice, and you made a poor choice by refusing to accept her apology and by not talking to her."

Joseph balled his fists at his sides. How could his mother come to his workplace and accuse him of—Suddenly his eyes filled with moisture. Embarrassed, he looked away. "What exactly are you getting at?" he asked when he found his voice. "What do you want me to do?"

"*Ach*. Finally, I get through that thick skull of yours." She clapped her hands together. "I want you to take this horse and wagon and go to the matchmaker's house and find Ruby. I want you to tell her that you have acted like a child and you're sorry."

"Sorry for what?" He lowered his voice to a harsh whisper. "She lied to me."

"She didn't tell you the whole truth. But what exactly did she say? Did she tell you that she was penniless?"

He thought for a minute.

"Did she?" his mother demanded.

He exhaled. "*Ne*, not exactly. But…we went

to see them. She let us think they lived in that little house. The garden was small. I naturally thought—"

"*Ya.* You assumed they were poor. But maybe this is partly your fault too. Maybe you didn't ask the right questions."

"M—"

Yet again she held up her finger and cut him off. "I've prayed on this. On my knees, I tell you. Sometimes I am too stiff-necked to listen when God speaks to my heart. We're human, Joseph. We make mistakes. Ruby made a mistake, but you made a mistake in refusing to listen to her. In hardening your heart against her."

"I was angry with her." He took a breath and then went on, quieter now. "I was angry and upset that she wouldn't trust me."

"And afraid that some fool would poke fun at you. Admit it." She took hold of his hand and gripped it tightly. "If our Father in Heaven can forgive our sins, how can you look at the woman you say you love and refuse to accept her apology? That is pride. And pride is worse than words. For such a human mistake, that a girl should listen to the advice of her parents and keep a secret from you, is that enough reason to ruin two lives?"

Heat crept up his throat. He could feel shame

rising in his chest. Was it true? Had he let pride come between him and Ruby?

His mother was quiet for a moment and then went on. "You have to decide who was wrong. Ruby? You? Both of you?" his mother continued. "You have to talk about it and you have to fix it. At least try."

"But you said she was all wrong for me. You said it was better if it ended."

"*Ya*, I did and I'm sorry for that. I hope you can forgive me. Both of you. I hope that in time I will be able to forgive myself for my selfishness. All I can say is that I thought I was saying what was best for you, when really what I was saying was what was best for me."

Joseph wiped his forehead with the back of his hand. "I can't believe you're standing here saying this to me," he managed.

She shrugged and gave him a half smile. "I can't either. Now, you take this horse and wagon. I'll drive your buggy home. And you go and try to straighten out the mess you have made of your courtship with Ruby." And with that, she walked across the yard to where his horse was tied. "James!" she called, waving her hand at him. "Come over here and hitch up this animal for me. There's no sense in me doing it. You're standing idle."

James put down his hammer at once.

"And you, Amos." Joseph's mother pointed at Amos. "Put your eyes back in your head and get back to work. My Joseph has more important things to do today than be a joke for the two of you."

Stunned, Joseph climbed up onto the wagon seat and gathered the reins. But he just sat there. Was she right? Was he as wrong as Ruby for not accepting her apology? Was what he had done worse than what's she'd done?

"Don't just sit there like a scarecrow!" Amos called good-naturedly to Joseph. "Do as your mother says."

Joseph did what any self-respecting man would do. He shook the leathers over the mare's neck and got out of there as fast as she could trot.

Chapter Fourteen

"Come on, *boppli*," Ruby coaxed the tiny fawn-colored calf. "Just taste this. You'll love it." She crouched down in the deep, sweet-smelling straw and held out the bottle. "It's delicious." The previous day, Leah's sister Grace had given her the little Jersey calf. Grace's husband, the local veterinarian, had purchased it for ten dollars from a farmer who'd intended to put the animal down. The mother had rejected the calf at birth, and without constant attention, the fragile baby had no chance of surviving.

Not only was this the wrong time of year for new calves, but this one had so far refused the nutrient-rich formula in the bottle. Getting the little Jersey to eat and keeping her warm in Sara's barn in the crisp autumn temperatures required Ruby's constant attention and around-the-clock feeding. It was a task that she had, at first, reluctantly accepted, but then she'd then thrown herself wholeheartedly into it. The calf, Star, as she'd decided to name it, needed her. And she needed something, other than Joseph's rejection, to concentrate on.

Star was so weak this morning that she could barely stand. Ruby had sat down in the oat straw and pulled the calf into her lap. With a clean towel, she rubbed the baby's coat, stroking and murmuring to the animal and scratching behind her ears. And when she felt the calf relax against her, she used up the last trick in her bag. From her pocket, she removed a half-pint mason jar of honey, dipped her fingers in it and rubbed the honey between Star's lips. For a moment, there was no reaction, and then a small rough tongue appeared.

"Ya," Ruby said. "It's good, isn't it?" The calf nudged her hand, seeking more of the sweet honey. Ruby dipped the nipple of the bottle into the honey and let Star suck on that. The tiny ears twitched and the tail wagged. The calf took the nipple and began to drink the formula. "Good girl, good *boppli,*" Ruby murmured. She pressed her face into the calf's warm neck, and for a few minutes forgot Joseph and her heartache and let the peace of the small creature in her arms sweep over her.

Footsteps pulled her from her reverie. She

glanced up to see Joseph standing at the edge of the stall. She blinked, not certain if he was really here, or if she'd imagined him.

"Sara said you were out here," he said.

She looked down at the calf. The bottle was half-empty. Afraid that Star would stop drinking if she got up, she remained where she was, concentrating on the calf in her arms. He pushed open the stall door and crouched beside her. She raised her head and gazed into his eyes. Her hand holding the bottle trembled.

"I've been a fool, Ruby," he said. "I'm so sorry. I… We should have talked. I should have listened to you. I should have…" He exhaled, gazing into her eyes. "Can you ever forgive me?"

She hugged the calf closer, wanting to believe that she was hearing what she was hearing. "*Ne*, Joseph, it was me," she whispered, tears filling her eyes. "I'm the one who was dishonest. It's my fault."

"Ruby, we were both wrong. You should have told me sooner. You should have trusted me. But I let pride and my mother's words come between us. My fault is greater."

"I didn't want…" she began. Then she stopped and started again. "I didn't know what to do, Joseph. My father said not to tell anyone. He said to find a man who would love me for me and not my father's dairy herd." She laughed because it sounded so silly now.

"It doesn't matter." He shook his head. "None of that matters. What matters is how we feel. About each other and…and I know how I feel. I love you, Ruby." He reached out and touched a wisp of hair that had escaped from her *kapp*. "I just hope you can see past my stupid—"

"Shh." Smiling at him through her tears, she pressed one finger to his lips. "No more," she entreated. "It was all a silly misunderstanding. If you really love me, it doesn't matter. None of it matters."

"I do, Ruby. I love you, and I want us to marry…to grow old together…to make our own family. If only you can…if only you could find it in your heart to—"

"Love you?" The bottle fell from her fingers. The calf bawled and scrambled to her feet. Ruby went to throw herself into Joseph's arms, but she leaned too far, hitting him in the forehead with hers. Down they both went into the straw. Joseph's hat rolled off, her *kapp* tilted to one side and her apron flew up over her shoulder, leaving one *kapp* string dangled across her face. "I do love you," she cried, laughing.

Joseph's lips, warm and firm, brushed hers, and sweet joy spread outward from his touch.

"Ruby! Joseph! What do you think you're

doing? Rolling in the hay? Kissing? In my barn? Shame on you both," Sara admonished.

They parted as quickly as they had come together, struggling to get to their feet. He offered his hand to her and pulled her up. Ruby straightened her *kapp* and pushed down her apron. Joseph brushed the straw off his shirt and retrieved his hat from the corner where the calf was happily nibbling on the brim.

Sara's eyes flashed. Her fists pressed against her hips. "What possible explanation do you have for this behavior?" she demanded.

Ruby covered her mouth with her hand and tried not to giggle.

Joseph moved to stand beside her. He pulled on his hat and then snatched it off to shake the straw out of the brim. "We—we want to be married," he declared. "As soon as the *banns* can be called."

"And you think that's an excuse?" Sara demanded. "For putting my reputation at risk? Not to mention your own?" She shook an accusing finger at the two of them. "Good for the both of you that I came when I did."

"It was just a kiss," Joseph explained. "Our first kiss, and there won't be any more. You have my word on it. I have too much respect for the woman who will be my wife."

Sara huffed. "A good speech for a young man

who not so long ago couldn't manage a single sentence without hesitating. Proof that all you needed was to find the right woman." She pursed her lips. "But a kiss has led to more than one regret. Kisses are best saved for the honeymoon. Do you understand, Ruby?"

"Ya," she said meekly.

"Are we quite clear on that?" Sara asked Joseph.

"Ya." He glanced down at Ruby, and his big hand closed over hers. "We'll try."

Ruby looked up, meeting his gaze, so filled with joy that it was hard to put two words together, let alone a sentence. "But maybe it's best if those banns are cried soon."

"My sentiments exactly," Sara said, turning and walking away. "Before your families cause even more mischief."

Epilogue

Ruby pushed aside the curtain to see the swirling snowflakes turning the fields and trees a wintry white. Outside, the temperature was dropping and the gray skies hung low over the house and barn, but she didn't mind. She liked winter. The small house was snug and toasty warm with its propane heat and the added comfort of the kitchen woodstove. The delicious smell of baking bread and simmering vegetable soup filled the downstairs.

She hoped Joseph would like the soup. Her cooking skills were not equal to her mother's and certainly not to Magdalena's, but they were improving. She and Joseph, together, had mixed up the yeast bread midday, and it had risen perfectly before she'd popped the loaves into the oven. It amused them both that Joseph had a real knack for making bread, biscuits and pancakes.

Baby Samuel, faithfully guarded by the tabby cat, was sleeping peacefully in his cradle. Ruby couldn't help smiling as she gazed at the small hand that had escaped the confines of his quilt and the tumbled mass of ringlets curled around his precious face. If she hurried, Ruby had just enough time to write a letter and put it out in the mailbox before Samuel woke from his nap and Joseph finished his wood chopping.

There were many things she could have been doing: diapers needed folding, the table had to be set for supper and there was that missing button on one of Joseph's work shirts that needed replacing. But keeping in touch with family was important, and she loved an excuse to sit at the small maple writing desk Joseph had given her on their second wedding anniversary. A horse and buggy passed the house on the road, the familiar rhythm of hoofbeats muffled by the falling snow. A family hurrying to get home before nightfall. That was another thing she loved about winter. Not that she didn't love her community and the constant coming and going, visiting and church services. She did. But days like this, when Joseph was home and it was just their little family, were special.

She took out a sheet of paper with a pretty flower border, found her favorite pen and began to write.

Apple Valley, Kent County, Delaware
February 14

Dearest Mother,
How good it was to see you last Sunday.
I'm so glad that you were able to get home
before the weather turned. It is snowing
here today, but we never get as much as you
do in Pennsylvania. Thank you for the baby
clothes. As always they are beautifully
sewn and the blue will look so nice with
his eyes. Joseph and I were talking, and I
think we are ready to move permanently to
Pennsylvania next fall when *Daddi* retires.
The good news is that we will be next door
to my parents and only a half hour away
by buggy from you. Joseph and I are so
happy that you and Elmer decided to move
to Lancaster to be nearer his daughter and
grandchildren.

It is our wish that Samuel and any other
children it pleases God to give us will grow
up with both sets of grandparents nearby
so that they will benefit from your wisdom
and love. We have found such happiness in
our marriage that we deeply want you and
dear Elmer to be part of it.

I know that you and I have had our differences in the past. I think we got off to

a bad start, but thankfully that is not the case anymore. Joseph and I have missed you since you married Elmer and moved to Pennsylvania. I do hope that you can give me some cooking lessons. I certainly need them. I made a vegetable-beef soup today, and I am hoping for the best. I remembered what you said and added a bay leaf and celery. I had red cabbage but no green, so…

The back door banged open and a red-cheeked Joseph stomped in amid a gust of cold air, his arms full of firewood.

Samuel startled in his cradle and let out a whimper.

"Sorry," Joseph called. He caught the door and pulled it closed before carrying the logs to the wood box beside the cookstove. "It's freezing out there."

Ruby jumped up and went to the cradle where Samuel was squirming. "Shh," she murmured soothingly as he opened one eye sleepily. "Hush, *boppli*. It's just your *daddi*." She rocked the cradle gently.

Joseph tugged off his gloves. "Did I wake him?"

She shook her head. "*Ne*, he's all right. He'll sleep a while longer."

"Goot." Joseph chuckled. "Let sleeping babies lie."

"Ya." She smiled at him. "Just look at our Samuel. He's growing by the day. He won't be a baby for long. Soon, he'll be trailing after you."

"And carrying wood." Joseph smiled at her as he shrugged off his flannel-lined denim coat. "Soup smells good."

She grimaced. "Don't say that until you've tasted it."

He returned the few steps from the living room to the kitchen and hung his coat on a hook by the door. "After living in this house, you won't know what to do in your father's big place," he said. "We'll rattle around like two peas in a pod."

"We'll have to fill it with children, I suppose."

He held out his arms and she went to him, laying her cheek against his chest and feeling the strength and goodness of him. *I'm truly blessed*, she thought. *I could not ask for a better husband.*

Joseph's arms tightened around her. "A round dozen, do you suppose?"

"Children?" She peered up at him. "A dozen?"

"Or more." He cupped her chin in his hand and raised it. "You remember what Sara told us?"

"What was that?" she asked. "I don't remember anything about twelve children."

"About the kissing," he teased as he lowered his mouth to hers.

Ruby closed her eyes and savored the tenderness in her husband's caress. "She said that kissing is for the honeymoon. And marriage."

"I agree," he murmured huskily. "But the last time I checked, we were married."

"So kissing's allowed?"

"Absolutely." He kissed her again. "Not only allowed by the faith, but encouraged."

She wrapped her arms around his neck and stood on tiptoe to kiss him again, a slow, sweet kiss of absolute, contented joy. And then she caught a whiff of burning bread. "Joseph! The bread!"

"Let it burn," he answered, still holding her tight. "This is more important."

And, she decided, it was.

* * * * *

If you loved this story,
pick up the other books in
THE AMISH MATCHMAKER *series:*

A MATCH FOR ADDY
A HUSBAND FOR MARI
A BEAU FOR KATIE
A LOVE FOR LEAH

And these other stories of Amish life
from author Emma Miller's previous
miniseries, HANNAH'S DAUGHTERS:

LEAH'S CHOICE
JOHANNA'S BRIDEGROOM
REBECCA'S CHRISTMAS GIFT
HANNAH'S COURTSHIP

Available now from Love Inspired!

Find more great reads at
www.Harlequin.com.

Dear Reader,

It's said that honesty is the best policy, but life is complicated. Can you imagine a situation where it would be better to hide things about yourself from someone you've just met? What if you've had a bad experience before and don't want to repeat the same heartbreak?

This is what happens when Ruby Plank comes to matchmaker Sara Yoder to find a husband. Ruby wants desperately to meet that perfect man who will value her for who she is. She isn't pretty, a good cook or a fine seamstress, but she's a good person who tries to live a Godly life. And she's the beloved only child of a mother and father she adores, parents who have advised her to keep a big secret.

The matchmaker isn't happy about the deception, but she's certain she can find a suitable match for good-hearted Ruby, even if she is a klutz. As usual, things don't go as planned, and when Ruby literally tumbles into the arms of shy Joseph Brenneman, knocks him senseless and sends him to the hospital, love blossoms. But the path of true love has a few bumps, and the mountain in this relationship is Joseph's formidable mother. From their first meeting, Magdalena distrusts the plain, chubby girl from

Lancaster County, and she won't give up until she puts an end to the courtship.

I hope you enjoy Ruby and Joseph's story, and I hope their love touches you as it has me. Come back and join us soon in the Amish community of Seven Poplars. I'm always happy to welcome new readers and old friends to life among the gentle people.

Wishing you peace and joy,
Emma Miller

Get 2 Free Books,

Plus 2 Free Gifts —

just for trying the Reader Service!

LIS17R2

Get 2 Free Books,
Plus 2 Free Gifts—
just for trying the Reader Service!

Love Inspired HISTORICAL

YES! Please send me 2 FREE Love Inspired® Historical novels and my 2 FREE mystery gifts (gifts are worth about $10 retail). After receiving them, if I don't wish to receive any more books, I can return the shipping statement marked "cancel." If I don't cancel, I will receive 4 brand-new novels every month and be billed just $5.24 per book in the U.S. or $5.74 per book in Canada. That's a savings of at least 13% off the cover price. It's quite a bargain! Shipping and handling is just 50¢ per book in the U.S. and 75¢ per book in Canada.* I understand that accepting the 2 free books and gifts places me under no obligation to buy anything. I can always return a shipment and cancel at any time. The free books and gifts are mine to keep no matter what I decide.

102/302 IDN GLWZ

Name	(PLEASE PRINT)	
Address		Apt. #
City	State/Prov.	Zip/Postal Code

Signature (if under 18, a parent or guardian must sign)

Mail to the **Reader Service:**
IN U.S.A.: P.O. Box 1341, Buffalo, NY 14240-8531
IN CANADA: P.O. Box 603, Fort Erie, Ontario L2A 5X3

Want to try two free books from another series?
Call 1-800-873-8635 or visit www.ReaderService.com.

* Terms and prices subject to change without notice. Prices do not include applicable taxes. Sales tax applicable in N.Y. Canadian residents will be charged applicable taxes. Offer not valid in Quebec. This offer is limited to one order per household. Books received may not be as shown. Not valid for current subscribers to Love Inspired Historical books. All orders subject to approval. Credit or debit balances in a customer's account(s) may be offset by any other outstanding balance owed by or to the customer. Please allow 4 to 6 weeks for delivery. Offer available while quantities last.

Your Privacy—The Reader Service is committed to protecting your privacy. Our Privacy Policy is available online at www.ReaderService.com or upon request from the Reader Service.

We make a portion of our mailing list available to reputable third parties that offer products we believe may interest you. If you prefer that we not exchange your name with third parties, or if you wish to clarify or modify your communication preferences, please visit us at www.ReaderService.com/consumerschoice or write to us at Reader Service Preference Service, P.O. Box 9062, Buffalo, NY 14240-9062. Include your complete name and address.

LIH17R2

Get 2 Free Books,
Plus 2 Free Gifts —
just for trying the *Reader Service!*

READERSERVICE.COM

Manage your account online!

- Review your order history
- Manage your payments
- Update your address

We've designed the
Reader Service website
just for you.

Enjoy all the features!

- Discover new series available to you, and read excerpts from any series.
- Respond to mailings and special monthly offers.
- Browse the Bonus Bucks catalog and online-only exculsives.
- Share your feedback.

Visit us at:

ReaderService.com

RS16R